D0827223

AN OVERCOAT:
SCENES FROM THE AFTERLIFE OF H.B.

Also by Jack Robinson
(a pen-name of Charles Boyle, editor of CB editions)

Days and Nights in W12

'Ingeniously observed, clever, elliptical and funny. It's like the
best moments from a novel – minus the padding.'
– Geoff Dyer

'It's about every urban space, including the one in your head.'
– Nicholas Lezard, *Guardian*

by the same author

'This book is a kind of portrait of the contemporary committed
reader: oh, you think, reading it, is *that* what I'm like?'
– Jonathan Gibbs

An Overcoat

Scenes from the Afterlife of H.B.

Jack Robinson

 editions

First published in 2017
by CB editions
146 Percy Road London W12 9QL
www.cbeditions.com

Drawings on cover, opposite title page and on pages 6 and 131
by Roger Barr (1921–2000), reproduced from Stendhal, *Memoirs
of a Tourist*, translated by Allan Seager, Northwestern University
Press, 1962; copyright reserved

Printed in England by T. J. International Ltd, Padstow

978-1-909585-24-9

ERRICO BEYLE

MILANESE

VISSE, SCRISSE, AMO

QUEST' ANIMA

ADORAVA

CIMAROSA, MOZART E SHAKESPEARE

MORI DI ANNO . . .

IL . . . 18 . . .

H.B., Milan, 1820:

"Every day I thought of this inscription, really believing that the
grave was the only place I could be at peace. I wanted a marble
plaque in the form of a playing card."

He had no belief in an afterlife, but one has to believe in it for him.

– F. W. J. Hemmings, reviewing a biography of Stendhal in the *London Review of Books*, 18 December 1980

The other one we are lives in a distant city.

– Frederick Seidel, 'Prayer'

Phrases within double quotes are the (translated) words
of Beyle/Stendhal himself (1783–1842), quoted from one
or other of the books listed on page 133.

I The Disguise

■ In June 1819 Henri Beyle followed the woman he loved from Milan to Volterra, in Tuscany, where she had gone to visit her children. He was thirty-six; he had written no novels, yet, but had published books on music and painting and the cities of Italy, making liberal use of writing by other authors, and he had met Mathilde Dembowski in Milan the previous year. Dembowski was aged twenty-nine and had two children and was separated from the Polish army officer she had married at seventeen.°

During the journey to Volterra Beyle put on green glasses and an oversize overcoat – the kind you might choose for shoplifting, with deep pockets; or the kind worn by SS officers in war films°° – so that he could observe Mathilde without being recognised, his reasoning being that if he greeted

---

° There are no known portraits of Dembowski. Beyle linked her to a painting in the Uffizi in Florence of Salome being presented with the head of John the Baptist; she is looking away, dreamily, barely aware of the waiter arriving with the glass of red wine she has forgotten she ordered.

°° Or a *carrick*, which Nabokov insisted was the correct English translation for the garment that furnished the title of Gogol's *The Overcoat*: 'deep-caped, ample-sleeved'.

her openly (a) she'd rebuke him for following her, and (b) everyone in town would assume he was her lover: "Therefore I shall show her far more respect by remaining incognito."

In January 1980 the French artist and writer Sophie Calle followed a man in Paris, lost him after a few minutes, then saw him again by chance that evening at a gallery opening, where he told her he was soon to travel to Venice. She followed him there, taking a suitcase in which she had packed 'a blond, bobbed wig; hats; veils; gloves; sunglasses'. In her account of the following days, the days of following, she names the man as 'Henri B'.

■ *Of course* Mathilde Dembowski saw through Henri Beyle's disguise. It was joke-shop, not even skin-deep. If you want to pass yourself off as a fishmonger, being able to tell a cod from a haddock might help; if you put on a dog collar, you should at least know your way around the Prayer Book. Actors, spies, fugitives, con-men and novelists who aspire to realism know this; as do people applying for jobs in which they've had no experience. But Beyle wasn't trying to be someone else, it was anonymity he was seeking, a harder thing;° or rather, he was seeking to be there but not have his thereness noticed, like an author with the kind of style

---

° "For me the supreme happiness would be to change into a lanky, blond German and walk about like that in Paris."

that gets called transparent. The man who had sold him his overcoat swore it was an invisibility coat. But it was second-hand, there were rips and stains, and some of the invisibility had worn off.

In 1819 Beyle retreated, chastised, and on 11 June he wrote a letter of apology to Mathilde; he longed to hate her, he claimed, but couldn't. When Dembowski returned to Milan she refused Beyle as a lover but allowed him to visit her once every two weeks. They talked, according to the (imagined) maid who listened at the door, about books, music, politics° and love in the abstract. In 1820 Beyle completed the first draft of *De l'Amour* and sent it to France, where it was lost in the post for over a year.

■ In *L'Abbesse de Castro* – a late novella that Beyle based on a Renaissance manuscript – Giulio, a brigand, is determined to visit the woman he loves, Elena, whose father has locked her away in a convent. Giulio's captain offers advice "as to the best way of carrying out this amorous and military

---

° Dembowski was closely linked to the Carbonari ('the charcoal burners'), a secret society that sought to free Milan from Austrian rule. Beyle too was sympathetic to the Carbonari, but his consistently inconsistent behaviour led both the authorities and those plotting against them to suspect he was an agent for the other side, and in 1821, after arrests by "the idiotic police", he had to quit Milan for good.

undertaking": travel in disguise; "never confess your true name"; never tell the truth (and if "you see no advantage in any particular falsehood, lie at random"); do not approach the town directly, and "enter by the gate farthest from the road by which you arrive".°

Dissimulation. Many of the characters in Beyle's novels practise this. Julien in *Le Rouge et le Noir*: "If she sees how much I love her, I shall lose her." In society, Julien achieves success by expressing, with a certain wit, the opposite of what he believes (which is fun for a while but becomes tiresome: "Julien achieved such a degree of perfection in this kind of eloquence . . . that he ended up boring himself with the sound of his own voice"). Beyle too made a habit of deception: his multiplying pseudonyms; his books published with prefaces that disclaimed his authorship; his marginalia written in code. Everything he yearned for was locked away in a convent, and could only be attained by following elaborate rules of subterfuge – a tangle of desire and disguise.°°

° The captain's advice resembles those 'tips for writers' that trend on the net and sometimes fill column inches in the broadsheet books pages. Here's another tip: if you're planning to write about someone who existed in history, be wary. Once you put an actual person into a book, they become larger than life, because larger than death. They become monsters. Beyle knew what he was doing when he kept Mathilde out of his book on love.

°° Anita Brookner (*TLS*, 30 May 1980), after listing some of Beyle's handicaps in his pursuit of happiness – 'narrow and confined

To live as if one were a character in an over-plotted opera is essentially comic.° So are disguises. I'm pretty sure that anyone who dons a disguise – beard, forged papers; green glasses, overcoat – *expects* to be seen through.

■ In Beyle's own attempt to replay in writing the Volterra episode, which was also his first attempt at fiction – Mathilde is renamed Bianca, the would-be lover is Poloski, and between them there's a lesbian duchess – he got no further than the first chapter.

---

childhood, the eternal need to earn money and position and favour, stocky and graceless body (even in his twenties), thin hair and bad teeth' – approves his furious attempts 'to measure up to the rules of the game, even when [my italics] *there was no game being played*'.

° "In Milan the primary, if not the exclusive source of comedy lies in observing the antics of a man who has lost his way among the labyrinthine paths which lead to the object of his heart's desire."

II Almost Bucolic

I

■ People are worried, and orders have come down from on high, and now, on the way in, there are security checks. Could you open your bag for me, sir? says a man standing at a table – an entirely innocent table on which flowers or fruit would gladly delight – and Beyle rests his bag on the table and opens the flap. The man pulls a notebook forward, pushes a printed book back (*Mrs Hutchinson's Memoirs*, "it is one of my passions"), tilts a water bottle, looks down to the bottom of the bag (a crumpled receipt, a paperclip). He's satisfied. He closes the flap and as Beyle retrieves his bag the man smiles and nods, just slightly, a gesture which in other circumstances – walking into your office, say, at ten in the morning (late, there were delays on the Tube, not your own fault but still, you are at fault) and passing the regular guy on reception, who is on the phone to someone who has just said something funny, or rude – would indicate familiarity, recognition, but which here carries a hint of apology, is virtually a *shrug*: sorry, sir, it's just the way things are. He doesn't say, Have a nice day. He doesn't say, Enjoy your visit.

■ Dawn. They are weaving between trucks on the ring road, overtaking on the inside and out, and it's raining, not hard but the road is wet. The spray is blinding, the noise an enveloping silence. She screams aloud and doesn't hear a thing.

The motorbike has been 'borrowed' by the boy from his older brother. The trucks are packed with furniture, clothes, toys, the refrigerated ones with meat, fruit, yogurts, kidneys for transplant, who knows, and each of their drivers is thinking: *she's not even wearing a helmet*, they are expecting that within ten miles two police cars and an ambulance will speed by, blue lights flashing, and there'll be a jagged metallic mush on the verge and back-up, traffic slowing to look.

What's it like, being fifteen?

It's not *like* anything, she doesn't have anything to compare it to. Right now it is speed and wind and rain and her arms locked around a thin boy's ribs, her body falling parallel to the world, her face stinging like it's being scraped against a wall. Freeze frame.

■ It's good, Beyle suggests, that she feels no fear, because what is there to be afraid of?° The young are immortal.

° About death, Beyle thought, people made too much of a fuss. "One suffers, one is astonished at strange sensations which come upon one, and suddenly one suffers no more, the moment is past, one is

Beyle knows who the girl is. He's not sure if she knows who he is. Today, sitting at a café table, showing off her turquoise fingernails, she is wearing her mother's perfume. But they don't talk about her mother, they talk about whether she should get a tattoo and how on the net you never really know who you're talking to. Beyle tells her that once upon a time, before mobile phones, people were often connected on party lines, so that when you picked up you could find yourself listening in to conversations between strangers: plans for tonight, arguments about who's going to pick up the kids, seductions. You could even join in. It was like a radio phone-in. Or the internet, the girl says. Or the inside of your head, Beyle says.

Which side did you wear your sword? she asks.

The left, of course; easier to draw when you needed to defend yourself.

But if you were left-handed?

Beyle laughs. He asks the girl in turn about nail bars and scratch cards and the smiley people outside the shopping mall who tell him the planet is going to fizzle out, and soon, if he doesn't put some money in their buckets. He can feel the couple at the next table looking at him and their

---

dead." Death is like, he suggested, riding a boat "through the dangerous rapids under the bridge of the Saint-Esprit on the Rhône, near Avignon": the passengers on the boat talk about this place in advance, are afraid, come within sight, and very quickly they have passed it.

mean little words lining up in their pea-sized brains: he's 'old enough to be her father'. In fact he's old enough to be her great-great-great-grandfather. *Défense de cracher*, it used to say in the carriages of the Paris metro.

■ On the ring road there are two car dealerships, a bicycle factory, a furniture depository, a riding stable, a school for autistic children and a tile warehouse. Beyond the ring road, farms, fields and forests on hillsides said to be gently rolling.° The average temperature for June is 23 degrees C. The average age of the town's population is higher, but not much higher, than the national average. There is a prison, an opera house (June to September only), a Gypsy Bar,°° two cinemas and an Irish pub (there is always an Irish pub). There are shops selling hiking gear. There are cafés with

---

° Descriptions of the the countryside: "I find them so tedious to do." Beyle suspected that Walter Scott had a secretary who filled in the scenic descriptions. ("If it had been my lot to have a secretary, I'd have been another kind of writer. – We have quite enough of those, says the devil's advocate.")

°° The gypsies who play in the Gypsy Bar on Friday nights are not real gypsies, most of them. The Ray-Bans sold by the sunglasses-seller outside the station are made in China, they are not real Ray-Bans. Neither of the two rival lunatics in this town who claim to be Napoleon can back this up. The woman at the hotel reception desk is not a natural redhead. The flowers on the tables in the hotel's

free wi-fi and twenty-three churches and three fine bridges, the latter built at a time when the town was wealthy, before a trade route changed course or a precious resource became available more cheaply elsewhere or no longer precious at all, and it stuck at a certain size, as some lives do too.° There are ruins and litter bins and locker rooms and hotels to suit all pockets. In the main square there is a fountain into which tourists throw coins while making wishes. Not coins of much value, and the wishes in proportion: to win a football match, to pass an exam, to have a lie believed, to receive a reply to a message posted on a dating site. At least one woman in this town has recently split from her partner and is now wondering if that was the right thing to do. But what else could I have done? she asks herself, given

---

dining room fool no bees. The silver crucifix that Anna wears on a necklace is not *silver*. The woman in the station at the foot of the escalator is a projected hologram. The god or gods worshipped in the twenty-three churches of this town haven't been seen for a while. Identity fraud – more resources are being put into tackling this, the government claims: your safety and security are our paramount concerns. The secret police – everyone knows who they are.

° 'Here there's peace. Here the air is good. Here you can eat well. Here you can feed the gulls. Here you can hike in the mountains. Here you can go by funicular up the Chaumont (1170 metres) in thirty minutes. Here friendly policemen give you information. Here the shops are open until seven . . . Here you go dancing on a boat beneath a canopy. Here the nights are boring.' – Horst Bienek, *Bakunin: An Invention*.

that now she has no one else to ask. Ah, says a man wearing sunglasses and an oversize overcoat as he steps out of the station, the rain has stopped. (Maybe she should ask *him*?) Puddles are evaporating in the sunshine, waiters are setting out chairs at outdoor tables and wiping them dry with tea-towels, and the air feels uncommonly warm. The leaves on the trees are tiny mirrors flashing messages.

■ Walking into the sunlight, the man off the train blinks (behind those sunglasses): *now what?* A seller of beads and wooden statuettes and yet more sunglasses in the square outside the station approaches, offers marijuana in a stage whisper, and asks his name. Beyle, Henry Beyle. Among many others: pick a card, any card.° The name of the seller of marijuana is volunteered as John. Beyle doubts this: it's just part of his sales patter, he thinks; he will be Jean for the French, Jan for the Dutch, Hans for the Germans. Or his real name is so hard to pronounce for anyone not from his country, with its consonants delivered from so far back

---

° Beyle had more pseudonyms than the scholars can count, more than he could keep track of himself. Some were borrowed from other nationalities; some were aristocratic, some bourgeois, some romantic, some comic or plain silly. Think of them as internet usernames: Aubertin, Auguste, Alceste, M. de Léry, Baron Dormant, Baron Patault, Baron Chagrin, Dominique, Dimanche, Ch. de Saupicquet, George Simple, Old Hummums, Timoléon Brenet, Timoléon Tisset,

in the throat no one else has access to them, that he has settled on John at random, a name he's heard called out or read in a book. Or he was raised in a mission school and assigned his name by some misguided priest – but surely that hasn't happened for some time, not within the lifetime of this John, who Beyle reckons to be aged twenty at most? He will ask him.

■ How does Beyle love M? Helplessly, idolatrously, obsessively, never-endingly, unrepentantly, voraciously, wilfully, X-ratedly, zodiacally.°

Dom Flegme, W. Sterne Renown, William Crocodile, Poverino, General Pellet, Meynier, Ths. Jefferson, Horace Smith, De Cutendre, Comte Change, Polybe Love-Puff, A. L. Capello, P. F. Piouf, La Borde, Blaise Durand, Lavardin, Adolphe de Seyselles, Chappier des Ilets, Condotti 48, Rowe, Caumartin, Chapuis, Chinchilla, Fudger Family, Porcheron, Count Anders von Westwerb, Van Eube de Molkirk, Tombouctou, Smith & Co. Etc. A *tissue of deceit* begets freedom, and it was this that Beyle required: not a single alternative fixed point, but continuous metamorphosis.

° Tongue-tied as a fifteen-year-old from the provinces or yattering on, Beyle knew that he was *too much* in love. To Mathilde Dembowski, 11 June 1819: "I know that I talked a lot, that I gazed at you, that I played the antiquarian. If it was at this time that I committed failures of delicacy, this is very possible. I have no idea. All I can remember is that I would have given anything in the world to be able to stare at the green tablecloth."

And how does M respond? With tolerant amusement, until her patience wears thin.

What's *exrate*? M's daughter would ask, when she was smaller. Or *eye-doll*, or *zodiac*, all the words she hadn't yet learned, or had misheard. Patience is a finite resource.°

■ 'This is Hannah,' says the woman who is renting the apartment on the floor below, introducing her daughter to

---

° When she was a child, M has told Beyle, she was bored. Her parents took her to parties where the adults drank and smoked and told jokes and shouted and danced, and on those occasions she was especially bored. Once, they were sent to a bedroom where they watched *The Jungle Book*, and when the film ended and they opened the door the flat was empty, the adults had vanished, and when M told Beyle that he saw what he imagined the children saw: overflowing ashtrays, empty bottles, lipstick-smeared glasses, cigarette burns, stray bits of clothing, a shoe, an open window banging in the wind. Put your shoes on, there's bound to be broken glass on the carpet. He imagined that she lived at the time in a northern city by the sea, a port. (She didn't. She lived in a town Beyle had never heard of, but when she told him its name he was unaccountably excited.) The children wandered down to the quays and found an old football and began kicking it about, traffic cones and discarded jumpers for goalposts, the boys mostly, a dog yapping at their feet, growling when the ball rolled under a car, the girls looking on, shivery and getting hungry too, until the grown-ups returned – but what if they didn't return? What if the world from that morning on had no adults in it, just children?

M's son. He already knows two other Hannahs and as he grows up it is statistically likely that he will come to know more. Which is the real Hannah? This one?

She's not saying. She wears braces on her teeth.

When the boy tells his mother that he dislikes his own name and wants a different one, she calls his bluff: fine, she says, if it's really what you want, it can be changed by deed poll. Which is the name of a man who runs a liquor store in a small town in the American West and who doesn't suffer children gladly. And which confirms what the boy has already begun to suspect: that there is no unanswerable reason for him to be *him*, that it's easy as falling off a log to become someone else – a someone unlikely to be any more satisfactory than the him he presently is, but the temptation is to believe otherwise.

M herself is often asked if her name is spelt with an *h* after the *t* – the company name and the dot co dot uk are easy but they need to know whether that *h* or not, otherwise it will bounce back. (Bounce back off what? A cloud of unknowing.) And at times she has wondered how much of a difference one letter more or less would have made to the life that she has. Nothing radical – another bangle on her wrist, those earrings rather than these, that man rather than this, a perfume in a differently shaped bottle. A life just to one side. But the flutter of a butterfly's wings in New Mexico, she has read, can cause a hurricane in China. She can remember precisely where she'd first thought about the butterfly: a late summer afternoon, on holiday with her mother and her sister, overlooking a bend in a slow-moving river bordered by reeds, with a tourist boat and some rich man's sports boat making waves, and she can remember wanting those boats to be *working* boats, barges with cargoes of timber, coal, iron, one of them with a broad slack sail coloured a weathered red, boats from another era, and she can remember worrying at the same time about the way her aesthetic sense was developing. *Sepia* was too easy an effect.

■ On mornings when the town is shrouded in mist it takes a while for Beyle to remember who and where he is, let alone the day of the week. The umbrella leaning against the wash-stand – it's not his, is it? It's still wet.

Ah, people tell him, but if he'd been here *last* summer . . . People are often telling him he should have been here *before* – a decade ago, two decades: the parties, the booze, the drugs, everything so cheap.° Curious economics of remembered happiness.°°

° He *has* been here before, of course. The sound of music from an open window brings back "the sound of a flute which some shop assistant was playing on a fourth floor on the Place Grenette". When he tries to explain this, people think that he's paying their town some form of compliment. He's not, but he lets it go.

°° The retrospective bent, a hankering to push everything back in time: back to the 1970s, when I was in my twenties and making as much of a fool of myself as Beyle did with Mathilde, and the

16

He wanders the streets with a kind of low-level non-specific sexual hunger, a sweetness in the gut, passing lovers kissing in the street and glancing back: she's sitting on a railing with her legs spread wide, making room. We're all led by our dicks, Beyle says aloud, and a woman steps out of a shop and stares hard at his shoes. Has he stepped into some dog dirt? There is nothing wrong with his shoes.°

---

children wouldn't be held hostage by their iPhones. Back further, to the 1950s, before colour TV, when people burned coal to keep warm and stood to attention for the national anthem and everything was in black and white. As if a frame would lend coherence. Beyle himself was constantly pushing forward the date at which he had any hope of being read: 1880, 1900, 1935 . . . He *distrusted* the present. In *Voyage dans le midi de la France* he lists some prices ("excellent room at the Hôtel Casset, 1 franc; table d'hôte dinner plentiful but table companions unmannerly, 2.50 francs"), begs the reader's forgiveness but suggests this information may be of value "in 1880, if, however, this rubbish is still in existence then". Writing to Prosper Mérimée about his first novel, he explained that in his customary way of writing, which he termed "the black-on-white style" (*le genre noir sur du blanc*), honest depictions of sex were not possible, and promised he would be more explicit "in 2826, if civilisation continues and I return to the rue Duphot". There are days when Beyle and I pass each other on the street, unawares, walking in opposite directions.

° 'A friend of mine once read *La Chartreuse de Parme* by Stendhal: it inspired him; he determined to change the direction of his life; in the end he just went out and bought himself a new pair of shoes.' – John Gale, *Clean Young Englishman* (1965).

Stay here where M is, even though he can't be with her, or leave, to where she isn't? He doesn't even have that choice. In love, thwarted, ridiculous – the wind has changed direction and he is stuck here for ever.

In the early evenings he watches two waitresses closing up the café near the station. One of them, the blonde, the taller one, does the chairs – lifting, turning, placing them upside down on the tables. The other girl, whose name is Anna, covers the dishes of sandwich fillings with clingfilm and takes them out back to the fridge. Next, she's mopping the floor, dabbing the mop in and out between the legs of the table-trees, squeezing it down on the plastic drainage thing in the bucket as hard as if she's drowning some specific someone, likely a man, while the first girl cashes up and then stands in the open doorway and smokes a cigarette. Tall girl: chairs, cashing up and cigarette. Anna: dishes and mop. No swapping of roles. Then Anna brings out the bin-bags, the rubbish, and dumps them on the pavement, full stop.

■ When Anna's boyfriend comes to her directly after the opera they don't get to sleep until dawn and the man who lives in the flat below complains about the noise, but really it's not the noise, he just has a grudge against life. On her day off, Thursdays, she does the laundry, and the machines are in the basement and this neighbour waits for her there and if she hasn't got the right change for the machines he refuses to help her out, on principle.

On Thursday afternoons she visits her stepmother in a care home. Often her stepmother doesn't seem to know who Anna is, but the other residents, nearly all of them women and nearly all a bit loopy, are happy to see her, except the ones who just nod or drool. Men clock out earlier, don't they? And you could ask, what's the point of having the last laugh if no one's around to hear it? One of the women has a dog and they all love that dog, everyone except the staff, who hate it, and the reason they love that dog is because it's young and it's something you take pleasure in looking at – which they, the residents, are not, frankly, though they have some good stories to tell. One of them climbed Mount Everest, another was married to a bullfighter.

It's always warm in the care home. It's like a fridge in re-verse: keep the old dears at a certain temperature, otherwise they'll go off. Even the cold water is warm, the water in the little plastic cups they are given with the pills that speed up or slow down their lives (the pink ones, the yellow ones, the green, the blue). And the tea is warm, not hot, and you can't see where you spill it because the carpets and furniture are the same colour, weak tea. The heating is always on and the windows are locked in the closed position, presumably to prevent the residents from throwing themselves out, but why shouldn't they? Is there a law against jumping out of windows? They can't sue for negligence after they're dead, can they? Their families maybe, but most of them would be only too happy never to have to visit that place again.

■ The reason she hasn't returned his calls, M says on the phone, is because. And then a dog barks and Beyle doesn't hear the rest. Her dog, not his. Was that a dog? he asks. What dog? she says. The dog that just barked, he says. What dog? she says again, as if he hasn't just heard what he heard, or she hasn't heard him. I'm just trying to say, she says, and then more barking. It is of course perfectly reasonable for a woman on her own, when she answers the phone, to play in the background the recording of a dog barking. *Don't even think* . . . A lion, a walrus, but a dog is more plausible.°

The dog is switched off.

Beyle invites her to dinner. Or for coffee or a walk in the park or to see some art, whatever she pleases, maybe come to his room, or . . . She says she hasn't got her diary with her.

■ The hotel where Beyle is staying is full but oh – and here the eyes of the redhead at the reception desk light up – there's been a cancellation, and he can stay on. He can't help but take this personally.

He visits churches and the local museum and, needing more underwear, the shopping mall. He frequents a certain

---

° Half of the 'Beware of the dog' notices nailed to front gates are just for effect; there's no actual dog at all. Or the dog has died, a year or two ago or maybe three, time passes and people forget exactly when.

café where one of the waitresses is pretty. He buys postcards and wonders who to send them to. He discovers that in a town frequented by tourists it is hard to walk in a straight line. Tourists walk slowly and stop for no reason at all in the middle of the pavement, like children before the dawning of spatial awareness. They are encumbered by bags ('daypacks'), maps, guidebooks, banknotes and coins they haven't got the hang of; they don't speak the language and they have very little idea of where they are. For this reason Beyle takes them seriously.°

Frequently they stop to take photographs, and Beyle observes the space between the person taking the photograph, not always Japanese, and the person or persons they are photographing, and steps around it. This happens often on bridges, or terraces. A woman steps out to the edge of the terrace, leans against the railing and looks across the ravine to the red-tiled roofs and the hills beyond. She turns to let her partner photograph her, the view now behind her, and then they change places and there is another photograph, and then they see Beyle and offer a little mime and he takes their camera and they pose together at the railing, leaning into one another and holding their smiles, fragile as glass, as if the long exposure times of early photography

---

° Beyle introduced Stendhal to the world with a travel guide to Italy, published in 1817 and written by "M. de Stendhal, *officier de cavalerie*".

still apply; or because they owe it to themselves to enter the future looking at their best: see, grandchildren, we were happy, we were in love – and Beyle presses a tiny button. *Then* they relax.

Not that there isn't a moment, a private moment, a playful moment too because nothing is going to come of it, a little conceit on a sunny day, when the woman at the railing looks down rather than across, down into the ravine, and sees herself falling, catching on the ledges and the jutting rocks, her body unrecognisable by the time it hits the bottom; and the man too, if he has any imagination at all, which he may not.°

■ Beyle is woken up by a phone call informing him that he has won the Nobel Prize, posthumously, and then his phone *is* ringing and he wakes up for real and the phone stops ringing before he can get to it. The light in the room is making a low ratchety noise, like a cat about to cough up a furball. He forgot to ask: for literature or economics? So he turns over and tries to burrow back into his dream but mistimes his re-entry and this time he's riding across a field towards a band of French infantrymen who, now that he's

---

° "I was told once, walking along the clifftop at Dover, that a person of nervous temperament, standing on the very brink of a precipice, feels an irresistible temptation to jump into the abyss."

closer, turn out to be not French but Russian, or a huddle of cows keeping out of the wind,° and then he wakes up again.

He feels that he is being watched: by that ratchety cat? But the light is silent now. It's like *bottled* light, as you might bring back from your holiday a bottle of some local liqueur that on a winter night at home will taste sickly sweet, nothing like it tasted on the terrace by the sea. This light does what it's expected to do – there are shadows behind where it gets blocked – but is a little clotted, heavy, tired, which is understandable, given that it's been travelling from so far away and for such a long time and at such a ridiculous speed and with no notion as to where it's headed to or why.

The dim light from low-wattage bulbs, but also the too-bright light, especially with a hangover. All novels, declares Baron Patault, with his whiskery sideburns and with the stagiest of pauses just *here*, are about unrequited love.

■ The Baron is choking with laughter, so much so that Beyle thinks he might have a heart attack and die – except that he can't, because this is the afterlife, which is itself the joke.

° "a ploughed field that seemed strangely in motion; the furrows were filled with water, and the wet ground that formed their crests was exploding into tiny black fragments" – the battle of Waterloo in *La Chartreuse de Parme*.

The very idea – the Baron now swirling his brandy – it's absurd. A novel in the afterlife? You might as well set a novel in a prison from which no one can ever escape or is ever released, a prison in which everyone has been incarcerated for so long that no one remembers why they are there, what crimes they have committed, even whether they are supposed to be the prisoners or the guards, and the keys have been thrown in the river.° Because no one can die, the stakes are sub-zero. No going back but, equally, no going forward, because there is nowhere to go forward *to*. The afterlife is a white room with a door that swings one way only, entry no exit.°° Why doesn't Beyle forget the whole idea and become a fur trapper? Or an oligarch? Why make the afterlife so difficult for himself?

Because that's not how it works, says Beyle. It's not a *holiday*. It's not a *second chance*.

His eyes now accustomed to the gloom, Beyle looks around the room: faded dustjackets on the wall; cushions stuffed with rejection slips that crinkle when you sit on them; a yellowing poster for a panel discussion on 'the limits of realism'; a cabinet of quills said to have been used by Cervantes, or maybe Rabelais; the carpet an abstract of

---

° Julien Sorel, in *Le Rouge et le Noir*: "The worst of being in prison, he thought, is not being able to lock one's door."

°° Armance, in Beyle's first novel: "Is a nun allowed, she wondered, to have wallpaper in her cell?"

unspecified stains. This is his first visit to what feels like a drinking club or a gambling club or a club for exiles from a distant land who have washed up here, in the town of twenty-three churches and three bridges, and is in fact all of these and caters mostly for deceased writers.

Patault from the pulpit, rubbing it in, repeating himself:° you can't have a novel without death. Without death in the margins – the glimmer of death, the promise and pressure and tease and titillation and shadow of death, the *ending* of death – nothing matters. Without time, without history to pass through, there is no meaning.

But people *don't* die in novels, Beyle says, matter-of-fact.°°

You flick back to Chapter 2 and there they still are, in the bloom of youth.

You look up to your shelves and there they still are. Even when you don't look up to your shelves, there they still are.

And when you tell what happens in novels, you speak in the present tense – everything still in play, all options open, Raskolnikov quite capable of putting down the axe and going out for a walk to clear his head.

° There's a lot of repetition in the afterlife. And because everything happens in one everlasting breath, without past or future, not much variation in tenses.

°° Giuseppe di Lampedusa: 'In *La Chartreuse* people don't really die, they just withdraw by imperceptible steps towards incorporeal memory.'

But the Baron has performed one of his trademark shrugs and turned his back and is walking towards Maupassant and Robbe-Grillet and a woman wearing a green headscarf at a table by the jukebox. Colette? Anaïs Nin? Beyle thinks of joining them, but at this stage of the evening they're all just characters in other writers' books. Instead, he holds up his empty glass and tries to catch the eye of the barman, a barman more boy than man but who moves at the speed of a reluctant glacier and holds grudges. Does Beyle know this man/boy? Does he owe him money?

Writers were rarely good company; the ones here are riddled with the same prejudices they always had, and they smell like old dogs. But the brandy is excellent.

Over his third or fourth glass, Beyle turns the pages of a local newspaper: a woman struck by lightning twice, a sporting triumph; births and marriages and all the deaths by design or misadventure or just 'passed peacefully away'. The deaths of chivalry, the welfare state and the manufacturing industry in the north. The death of neoliberalism. The death of the novel. The death of the author.

Out of the blue, Beyle feels uncommonly refreshed.

■ Eleven years old, this boy who's always going missing on school trips: still in the toilets at the service station when the coach rejoins the motorway, still on the metro when the rest of the class are lining up on the platform and the doors close.

Relationship with his sister: complicated. Relationship with his mother: off-and-on. Relationship with his father: n/a. He wonders, of course he does, if his parents are really his parents; he has an inkling that it is all, at some level no one ever talks about but isn't hard to fathom, a *mistake*.

His mother thinks he's lonely. His mother thinks that loneliness is a disease, like chickenpox or German measles, and she blames herself for having missed an appointment for the vaccination.

He likes watching people who are doing repetitive work – cashiers at supermarket checkouts, scaffolders, soldiers, street-sweepers, married couples, writers. Within his own lifetime, he believes, there will be machines to perform any task that humans need to be performed, and then there will be no need for humans, so no need for tasks, but the machines will carry on performing whether need or not. Elimination of human error: eliminate humans.

He fails to understand why it's assumed that after dying you go to a *better place*.

He likes days like today – showery, blustery, short-tempered.° He likes staring at girls until they become uncomfortable, crossing and recrossing their legs, and then

---

° The bridge over the estuary is closed to high-sided vehicles. On beaches a hundred miles away, black flags fly. A windy day is a potent thing, especially when the wind comes from the nor'-nor'-east. Grit in your eyes, flurry of litter in the alleys. Seagulls are blown inland. Nothing stays where it's put, there's shuffling in the streets

cross. He likes going into the Hotel Aramis and sitting in the lobby and thumbing around on his iPhone until Beyle too becomes twitchy. In a shop selling outdoor gear he tries on a puffy jacket and talks with a sales assistant about the difference between 'waterproof' and 'weather-resistant'. Have you got any flares, he asks? Those things you light and send up high into the sky when you're lost? They are pretty. They *are* pretty, she agrees, but shakes her head. They do stock them, in the basement, but she's not going to sell them to this underage boy.

Here, on the stand near the door, are fleecy gloves. Here are packs of hooks for hammering into cliff faces and tents and sleeping bags and thermal blankets and knives with many blades and GPS gadgets that tell you exactly where on this spinning globe you are. The last have the appeal of a conjuring trick. With a gadget he's nicked from another aisle he clips a chain, slides a GPS thing off its stand and into his pocket and walks out. The world is so elaborately

---

and around the next corner you could easily come across a jumble of blown-off ears and noses all piled in a heap, a *dune*, and a beggar sorting through them for something edible. A name – you thought it was yours and now it's someone else's. You're in love, then turned about in terror or indifference. Chronology gets in a tangle, gender too. You take your life in your hands but it's twisting and flapping and escaping your grip. Never, ever, should a pregnant woman go outside on a windy day: a sudden gust can turn you inside out. Then the wind changes to southerly . . .

geared to making you want things that when you don't want anything you become invisible: there's a loophole here, another conjuring trick, and he's found it.

When the boy grows up, Beyle thinks, watching the boy fiddling with his iPhone in the lobby of the Aramis,° he will either die young or become very, very rich.

■ It's not hard, de Saupicquet once told me, to gain entry into other people's lives: they generally leave the spare key under the plant pot by the back door, the usual place. But once you're in, it hits you that they have gone out, and you have no idea when they'll be coming back.

■ M's sister: she is difficult, M has warned. She blinks more than is normal. She gets migraines. Flash-light hurts, and sudden noise. She asks you to repeat what you've just said, a way of slowing things down, and then echoes your last words before replying. There's nothing wrong with her hearing. She has left her lover, or vice versa, and, always fragile, she is cracking up, which is the reason M is now visiting. When they were children, M has told Beyle, her sister made everyone's life a misery by going into a sulk if

---

° We'll get to the Aramis. "Nothing is more difficult in this solemn tale than to respect chronology."

she didn't get her own way. Because this worked, or because the wind changed direction, she kept the sulk, and people fall for it, hypnotised by that blinking. They behave towards her as though she has suffering in her life – her parents were killed in a car crash, or she has some deep-set illness that's too awful even to ask about. Grief is involved. Or maybe she's a saint. She is not a saint, M says.°

■ Staring at the straight-as-a-die cast of a Roman road, Beyle suffers an acute attack of vertigo.°°

° Beyle had two sisters, one of whom, Pauline, he was deeply fond of: "I'd marry another Pauline if I could find one who wasn't my sister, even if it meant earning a living as something, a printer for instance, a newspaper hack or something even more dismal." His letters to her are full of affection, reading lists, encouragement of her desire for independence and worries about her free-spiritedness: dressing up in men's clothes, he advised, might be fun but hardly enhanced her marriage options. And marriage, for a woman, in the time they were living, was crucial: "A woman needs to be married, first and foremost; it's what people ask of her; after that she can do what she wants."

°° "This morning, 16 October 1832" – Beyle beginning his memoir, *La Vie de Henry Brulard* – "I found myself at San Pietro in Montario, on the Janiculum Hill in Rome; it was gloriously sunny. A light, barely perceptible sirocco was causing a few small white clouds to float above Monte Albano . . ." The clouds are a nice touch and all is proceeding neatly, time and place exactly noted, but in fact(?) it

■ M is late, but no later than is her right. She hasn't dressed for dinner – flat heels, minimal make-up – and nor is she conciliatory. She is furious with Beyle for still being here. People are looking, people neither of them will ever see again. She accuses him of an 'invasion of privacy' and then, annoyed with him, or me, for saddling her with such terrible lines, tells Beyle that he is no better than a stalker,

---

was three years later that he wrote that sentence and under a different sky. In the same paragraph he recalls being present at the battle of Wagram in 1809, when "my friend, M. de Noue, had his leg taken off". A few pages later he admits that he wasn't properly in the army at all (he was "an assistant in the War Commissariat, a post reviled by the soldiers") and certainly wasn't at Wagram (he was lying ill with syphilis in Vienna on the date of the battle) – but, addressing his readers forty-five years in the future, in 1880, he notes that he is writing at a time when it is "fashionable" to have served under Napoleon and so "it is a falsehood altogether deserving of being written to let it be understood indirectly and without absolute untruthfulness (*jesuitico more*) that one was a soldier at Wagram".

Beyle's way (the usual adjective is 'cavalier') with facts is also that of Ford Madox Ford, whose preface to his own first book of memoirs warns: 'This book, in short, is full of inaccuracies as to facts, but its accuracy as to impressions is absolute . . . I don't really deal in facts.' To the reader who spots the greatest number of inacurracies, he offers a copy of the ninth edition of *Encyclopaedia Brittanica*, 'so that you may still further perfect yourself in the hunting out of errors'. He mentions that he happens to be writing 'in Bloomsbury at this moment', then later adds, *à la* Beyle: 'I find that I have written these words not in Bloomsbury, but in the electoral district of East St Pancras. Perhaps it is gloomier in Bloomsbury. I will go and see.'

and his use of her as an object on which to project his desires is basically pornographic. That she looks so desirable when she is angry is such a cliché that Beyle is already defeated. She tells him to go, *now*. She knows that the last train has already left but there must be taxis to the capital and flights from the airport, they're not stuck in the nineteenth century. Beyle says the twentieth would be worse. They are in

---

In another preface: 'When it has seemed expedient to me I have altered episodes that I have witnessed . . . The accuracies I deal in are the accuracies of my impressions. If you want factual accuracies you must go to . . . but no, no, don't go to anyone, stay with me.'

Beyle, the Anglophile Frenchman who wrote under a German-flavoured name; Ford, the Francophile Englishman who started life with a German name and then changed it to an English one, and who wrote what Graham Greene called 'the best French novel in the [English] language' – cousins, surely? Both men saw active military service (Beyle with Napoleon's army during the invasion of Russia and the retreat from Moscow in 1812, Ford in the trenches in World War One). In looks, neither was much to write home about, yet both 'had Goethe's gift for picking a bright girl' (Robert Lowell on Ford) and led tangled love-lives.

Both Ford and Beyle were also incapable, in both their lives and their writing, of doing anything in a straight line. Ford drifts through a series of historical novels before getting into his full stride with *The Good Soldier*, whose time-shifts and style are true to the spirit of meander: 'I have, I am aware,' Part Four of the novel begins, 'told this story in a very rambling way, so that it may be difficult for anyone to find their path through what may be a sort of maze. I cannot help it.' Beyle begins with books on music and painting

the dining room of Beyle's hotel, and he recommends the octopus cooked in a kind of chilli sauce.

'Maybe we should just fuck,' M suggests, as if reading aloud from the menu might offer some clue as to what these dishes might actually *taste* like. 'We're already in a hotel, you have a room. The lift is just over there' – for a moment Beyle is completely sure that she means this, and for a moment she does mean it, but it's not the same moment – 'and then you could get on with the rest of your life, and me

---

largely plagiarised from other writers. He is determined to become a comic dramatist, but never finishes a single play. He writes a novel whose main character is impotent and hides this fact so artfully that everyone is puzzled, not least the girl. Eventually, a chance newspaper crime report propels him into writing *Le Rouge et le Noir*, and he's off, but with characteristic indirection: plots that double back on themselves, narrative perspectives that veer between first-person and third-person, and a style that both affects to be and sometimes is careless.* Dates and directions and the ages and circumstances of his characters are unstable: in *La Chartreuse de Parme* he has a character in 1822 reading a book that wasn't published until 1837; in the same novel Count Mosca has a wife and then, conveniently, not. Famously, Beyle compares his novels to mirrors carried along a road – but, as Michael Wood puts it, 'the mirrors tilt, jump and go dark with alarming frequency'.

* 'A road running southward from Parma cannot possibly lead to Sacca and the Po, which lie to the north.' – from the Appendix in Robert M. Adams, *Stendhal: Notes on a Novelist* (1959), listing (good-humouredly) 'some of the major slips, inconsistencies, oversights'.

too.' She goes back to the menu. But that wouldn't work, she says, because what he's really in love with is his suffering. He despises the kind of love he calls mannered but he thrives on it. 'Every glance, every blush . . . It's geekish. Voyeuristic. Adolescent.'

Beyle defends himself by saying pornographic maybe, but quality porn, *literary* porn, and about the desires that she mentioned there is nothing unnatural, and even if she isn't interested in him as a lover she can't help but be interested in his being a writer – they had met at a literary salon – but line by line the conversation peters out. He looks at her buttons, she stares at his chin.

How are her children? Beyle asks. How is her sister? How was the octopus?

'Everything we've said has already been said by everyone else in this room,' M remarks.

Beyle points out that the dining room is now empty.

It's not, M says. There's at least one other person, Beyle's idea of herself, quite different from her real self, who Beyle can't see through to because he's erected this *idea* in her place. Flattering, but hardly original. Besides, over there by the door to the kitchen – see – there's a waitress and two waiters.

They don't count, Beyle says; they are bored, they just want to clock off and go to bed. Or two of them want to go clubbing and one wants an early night. I'll get the bill.

■ Caumartin has realised that he's in love with Angela (how did it take him so long?). He finds it possible to believe that she is in love with him. He hasn't slept with her yet but today is the day: her flatmates are away for the weekend at a festival and she's asked him round. At six o'clock he's a little nervous: he keeps feeling he needs to pee, only to find, when he goes to the toilet, that he doesn't. Something is at stake here. After will never be the same as before, he knows this; or it will be the same but minus the wondering, so the same but in a different way.° He checks the weather forecast: clear skies, no rain, temperatures rising. He showers and chooses what to wear and then changes his mind, but he needs to buy flowers and he's already running late.

No signal failures, no roadworks disrupting traffic, he takes as a good omen – the gods approve – but he arrives more than half an hour early. So this is where she lives: on an island surrounded by a river teeming with flesh-eating piranhas which he has valiantly to cross. Or a street of ter-raced houses, trees, more upmarket than he'd expected, to judge by the cars parked along the kerb. He stands outside number 42 and looks up. It's ill-mannered to arrive early. She's forgotten and has gone away with her flatmates to the

---

° Beyle in the army after coming under fire for the first time, "a sort of virginity weighing as much on me as the other": "What, is that all there is to it?" Julien in *Le Rouge et le Noir*, after making love for the first time: "*N'est-que ça?*" Lamiel in *Lamiel*, after hiring a man to take her virginity: ditto.

festival, or forgotten and then suddenly remembered and gone out to buy food. He should have offered to bring the food himself.

He goes to the pub at the end of the street, at the junction where he got off the bus. An ambulance speeds by, siren blaring, blue lights flashing. He orders a beer. A man with one eye on the blink offers him a smartphone, brand new, *in its box*, bargain price, and then says that he has killed eleven people but he was in the army when he did it so maybe it doesn't count, maybe none of them count. Where was this? Beyle asks. In the desert, it was hot. How hot? Hot as hell, the man says.

When Caumartin comes out of the pub the sky is dark and cars have their headlights on. A light rain is falling. His feet shuffle leaves on the pavement. Under the street lights, the colours of the flowers he is carrying are not what they were.

■ Reprise. Beyle and M are having dinner again, or are having the same dinner but with a second bottle of wine. M knows that Beyle has a book in mind and that it's not a novel, more a kind of essay, and she approves. Stories, she says, are hindsight, retrospective. We are storyed out. We are *backed up* with stories. And anyway, people today don't have the time for stories, they want to cut to the point: 'They want to be told how to live their lives, they want *advice*.' The author as agony aunt.

I want to disagree, and draw up a chair at their table. I talk about reading from wherever a novel falls open, a dipping-in-and-out no less valid than reading *in a straight line*. M laughs: it's how people read the *LRB*, she says. Well, yes – here the one remaining waiter approaches and offers me a menu: thank you but no, I'm just stopping by, I'm not staying – but even if the narrative tra-la is just scaffolding it's still story that delivers the best *sentences*. M rolls her eyes. Beyle asks if I've read Flaubert's letter to Louise Colet in which he spoke of writing 'a book about nothing, a book . . . held aloft by the internal force of its style, as the earth stays aloft on its own'. He seems pleased with himself for remembering that quote; I think he is tiring, has reached his limit.

I'd like a whisky now, but our waiter has disappeared. I take a bottle from behind the bar and a glass from one of the empty tables and pour myself a generous measure (this is *my* book, after all). M wants a whisky too, and asks if there's any ice. There is no ice. She once worked as an intern in the marketing department of a trade publisher, and is still enthusiastic about Beyle's new book having an instructional point. I'm beginning to go off her: at heart she's just another puritan, one of the tribe that insists that literature is *good for you*. Despite her belief that people have less time to read than they did,° she disapproves of skipping; she believes you

---

° Not true: life expectancy in the West is now longer than it was in the days of triple-decker novels, we have more time.

should always finish a book, even though we know that endings are often the weakest bit; and it's against the rules to jump to the last page to see who's been killed off and who lives happily ever after.

Beyle's book, M speculates – I pour her another whisky – and though she suspects it is about love, which is what Beyle goes on about, she has no intention of interfering, except to demand that she herself be kept out if it – a condition that in 1819 Beyle agreed to: *De l'Amour*, though taking its whole charge from his relationship with Mathilde Dembowski, contains no mention of her° – Beyle's book, to give this sentence back its subject, might get onto the reading lists for students at colleges, might even become a *set book*, in which case he would become rich. And thereafter he'd be able to have any woman he wants, or so the story goes, but I doubt that. Beyle shrugs.°°

° In 1923 the Russian writer Viktor Shklovsky, living in exile in Berlin, fell in love with Elsa Triolet. She allowed him to write to her, but on this condition: 'Don't write to me about love. Don't. I'm very tired.' The result was a book (*Zoo, or Letters Not about Love*) of letters from Shklovsky to Triolet about animals, cars, cities, trousers, books, earrings, the weather, writers' gossip, laughter – in sum, about love.

°° By his own count, seventeen copies of *De l'Amour* were sold in the eleven years after its publication. His first novel, *Armance*, published in 1827, fared no better.

■ We don't love one another, do we?° *The child's father is absent.* He went to meet me at the station, but I did not see him. *I was asleep in the back of the car; I saw nothing.* I saw him at a quarter to four. *I have just come from Isfahan; is there a good hotel in this town?* He said that truth was the most important thing. *It is not usually like this in spring.* The streets are dirty because it has rained a lot. *I came here to call on you, and your servant said you had gone out.* I never thought of looking for him behind the door, I must admit. *Can it be done or not?* He kept on and on talking, most eloquently, I admit, but in the end I grew tired. *Will you permit me to come with you?* Whatever his merits may be, he always has very dirty hands. *If there is work for a labourer, give it me.* It is difficult to understand why he wanted us to go to bed so early. *I have given you much trouble.* He said it was very hot, but I was cold. *I am sorry; I was rather ill, through eating bad meat.* The water was so hot that he had to wait ten minutes before taking his bath. *Actually, there is no water.* I am trying to find a place that isn't wet, as I want to sit down. *If I had known that it would be like this, I would never have come.* His younger sister is very inquisitive. *Perhaps I will come back tomorrow.* It is not yet certain that there has been a revolution. *You always tell lies; the road has many holes.* Don't

° Alternating sentences are from (roman) *Classified Revision Exercises in Spanish* by E. Hart Dyke and W. E. Capel Cure (George G. Harrap & Co. Ltd, 1932) and (italic) *Colloquial Persian* by L. P. Elwell-Sutton (Routledge & Kegan Paul Ltd, 1941).

speak to me in that way; speak to me more politely. *I have been driving in Iran for several years, and I have never seen a road like this.* I don't think he can have heard what I said. *I want three yards of green cloth.* I believe he bought this for me, but it will be useless. *It is made entirely of silk.* How much I meant to do, and how little I have done! *Where is there a butcher?* Look for him outside; he's not likely to be under the table. *He has not been killed.* Who is it that is calling us? It is we. *There is a lot of dust on this table.* He put on his overcoat and went out.

2

■ 'When M refused me,' Beyle tells Anna, 'I died. And then, of course' – not wanting there to be any misunderstanding between them – 'I did die. Officially. In 1842. On 23 March, at two in the morning.'

She ponders this. He does look a little pale.

He is hoping that putting his cards on the table will explain why he may seem a little *distrait*. And convince her that for all practical purposes he is as normal as anyone else.

She asks him what dying is like, a good question, and he'd like to answer her but he can't, because at the time of his death, the one for which a certificate was issued, he'd been unconscious for several hours.

She's disappointed: a wasted opportunity.

Anna is tone deaf, her boyfriend has told her, and he's right. In return, she has told him that he's been checking off files at the opera magazine for too long and it's time he wrote some of the reviews himself. Or a libretto, even – for an opera set in a care home. Climactic scene of the first Act, just before the interval: villainous corporate profiteers beset by a chorus of underpaid care workers. He looked at her blankly. She doesn't think he should go on stage – he doesn't have the right figure, he's too skinny. Her figure and

41

his voice, that might work. It's a shame they can't swap a few genes. What does Beyle think?

One day soon she'll move to another town, Beyle tells her, and then her Thursdays and her boyfriend will be different.°

Meanwhile, she is brimming with more questions. In martinis, gin or vodka better? Can fish drown?°° If animals have feelings, why not vegetables? Why do children like climbing trees? What exactly is wrong with enlightened despotism? Terrorism: will there be more or less of it in the future? Should we live every day as if it's going to be our last, or can we be a bit more relaxed about this?

Without really thinking about it, Anna assumes that Beyle, having moved on from this place of ignorance, pain,

---

° Beyle and waiters/waitresses have history. In *Voyage dans le midi de la France* he rants about the waiters of Marseilles, Lyons and Bordeaux; he carries his tea leaves with him and asks just for hot water, and "the reader will have perhaps noticed my habit of measuring the degree of civilisation by the degree of hot water I am served". Impossible to know whether the waiters – who generally served him a "sort of lukewarm concoction" – were in fact toying with this stranger from out of town, or taking revenge for his grumpiness, or just refusing to be rushed. Waitresses, on the other hand: "The young woman leant forward over the bar, which gave her the chance to show off her wonderful figure. Julien saw this: *all his ideas changed*. This beautiful girl came to put a cup, some sugar and a roll in front of him." (*Le Rouge et le Noir*; my italics.)

°° Yes, if there's not enough oxygen in the water.

42

decrepitude and random moments of bliss, knows all the answers. This is an illusion, but not a dangerous one.

■ He presses the button for 'balance on screen' and stares hard at the figures, willing them to change. They don't.

Beyle's money is running out.° He needs sponsorship. Or a job as an instructor at the riding school on the ring road ("a life of falling in love and off horses"). Or as a consultant on any film that's set in the period of the July Monarchy; or even as an extra, in an ill-fitting costume. Nothing get-rich-quick, nothing that will draw attention to himself ("I'm happy in an inferior position. Perfectly happy, especially when I am hundreds of miles away from my employer"). Or he could self-harm, just enough to keep him safely tucked up in a hospital bed with a book and worry about the money later;°° or get himself arrested – for identity fraud? – and live if not well then at least for free off prison fare.

Instead, he checks into a cheap hotel that has only enough

° Beyle's money was always running out. He hoped for a fortune when his father died but inherited only debts. He made very little from his writing, nowhere near enough to live the life he wanted.

°° After the debacle with Mathilde: "I arrived at the Saint Goth-ard Pass, which was in an abominable state then (exactly like the mountains in Cumberland in the North of England, with precipices added). I wanted to cross it on horseback, rather hoping I would have a fall and take so much skin off I would be distracted from

space in the lift for two people, often just one, because it is a hotel for tourists on tight budgets and many of these arrive with rucksacks half the size of themselves. Its location is good, directly opposite the café where Anna works.

By the end of the week, Beyle has moved into the hotel's smallest room, more cupboard than room, which he gets free in exchange for working behind the reception desk for a few hours each day. There is space for just a single bed and a washbasin and a small dressing table but there is time galore, time in spades, afterlife time, time to kill. On plastic chairs on the tiled floor in the hotel lobby he plays chess with Franco, who may or may not be the acting manager and who also works as a tour guide. They play on a pocket-sized board which a tourist has left behind and substitute a small Turkish coin for a missing bishop, and then a button when they lose the coin.

---

other matters." Suicide,* in the afterlife, is not an option, but in Beyle's previous life he considered it more than once: "In 1821 I had great difficulty in resisting the temptation to blow my brains out. I drew a pistol in the margin of a bad play about love I was writing then." What stopped him on that occasion was "political curiosity"; and – "perhaps, also"– it might hurt.

* Emmanuel Carrère tells of the suicide attempt by Edvard Limonov, prompted by his reading of *Le Rouge et le Noir* – a book which he loved, but which on second reading made him realise the wretchedness of his own life: knowing no 'beautiful aristocrats' and having no chance of ever meeting any. He cuts his wrist, watches his blood soak into the book, and 'wakes up the next day in the nuthouse'.

Beyle has come down in the world, but not as far as a raccoon or a tsetse fly.[°]

■ Without his SS overcoat and his sunglasses, Beyle is non-descript. Medium height, dark jacket, brown shoes, tattoo of an angel on his left forearm – but no, if he is wearing a jacket I must be thinking of someone else. I can't even describe myself, beyond bad teeth. In the event of what the police like to call an incident, I'd be so stutteringly incapable of describing any person in any detail that my own name would immediately be added to their list of suspects.

The plumber, for example, who has come to unblock the toilet on the third floor: a man so large and ungainly that it is hard to imagine how he could ever duck tight beneath a sink to replace a U-bend. A lump of pumice stone, but heavy as lead. Taciturn, short of language, so everything has to be conveyed through his sidekick, who is much younger and has a high-pitched voice. Or, at the jewellery shop where a necklace has caught Beyle's eye, the man behind the counter who is clean and fresh and unused. Hygienic. His white shirt still has the creases from how it was folded in the box in which it arrived. He is besotted by very small things, one and then the next. His eyes are set far back in

---

[°] Nabokov (in *Nikolai Gogol*): 'You will first learn the alphabet, the labials, the linguals, the dentals, the letters that buzz, the drone and the bumblebee, and the tsetse fly.'

his skull and Beyle worries about this, though there is probably no need. Years ago, when he pulled a face or looked upset, Maria would tell him to stop it at once because if the wind changed direction he'd be stuck like that for ever. Maria was not an imaginative person; she was simply repeating what she'd been told herself as a child. Beyle asks for a discount and the man gets confused.

■ There are, Anna has read in a magazine, *round* characters, who behave in a 'realistic' way and who are capable of psychological development, and there are *flat* characters, who are dimensionally challenged, and Beyle suggests that if she is planning a party it's probably good to invite both kinds.°

Which am I? Anna asks Beyle.

You decide, he tells her. You choose.

Anna thinks Beyle should smile more. Hard to love a man who's not ticklish.°°

° In 'A Singular Occurrence' by Machado de Assis two flat characters mistakenly assume that the mistress of their friend – a polite, obliging woman who 'had quiet manners and never swore' – is also flat. One night she goes out into the street and picks up a stranger, a self-confessed 'good-for-nothing', and has sex with him. Bafflement as to her motivation – 'accident, God and the devil rolled into one . . . Well, who knows?' – is at the centre of the story.

°° "I smiled little so as not to seem ironical."

You don't have to decide right now, he tells her. There's plenty of time.

■ A glass smashes in the next room, or maybe a mirror. Smallest of pauses – a drag on a cigarette while talking – then the voices of the very tall Swedish couple at full pitch again. Some useful insults and cuss words in there, Beyle thinks, if only he knew the language.

Meanwhile, in the conference room – everyone sitting in rows, it's like being back at school – love and lust in the afterlife are being debated for the umpteenth time. If neither, why bother? If yes, what makes the afterlife so different from actual life? Apart from death being taken out of the equation – but most people most of the time behave as if there will always be a tomorrow, so not much difference there. To reduce congestion, a plan for a bypass from conception direct to the afterlife is being considered.

Observing the delegates in their albs and their cassocks and their chasubles and their skullcaps, 98 per cent of whom are male, Beyle wants to put up his hand and ask what gives *them* the right to decide. How can they possibly *know*? They might more usefully be discussing – though attendance would be down – how to raise funds to mend the holes in their roofs. On the other hand they seem friendly enough, they can do small talk as well as the capital letters, they've commissioned some very fine music and art, so maybe they're not as stupid as some of the things they come out with. It might help if they all spoke in Aramaic; priests are always more impressive when you can't understand what they're saying. Beyle tries to imagine himself as one of them, wearing a loose-fitting alb, a garment so pure and simple it would be a shame to get it in a twist.

He's in a twist himself. He thinks about M's sister, who is gay, and the waitress Anna, who is not, and M, and about why this woman rather than another. *That* is the question.

Through a sultry week in early spring, the sun never quite breaking through, the conference drifts along with coffee breaks and guest speakers and reports from subcommittees on marriage.° But everyone has shopping to do, deadlines to meet, this life as well as the next. In the final session the usual compromise resolution is reached, the best they can do without causing offence: yes, there will be sex in the after-life, but *not as you know it*. After lunch on Friday the delegates fill in their expenses claims and head off to their wives, mistresses and monasteries, and the cleaners move in.

About the state of the rooms left by travellers in the Hotel Aramis, Franco has opinions verging on racist: the Japanese fold their sheets neatly, the Australians leave theirs in

---

° If you are married when you die, are you still married in the after-life or is the slate wiped clean? If still married, how long should a predeceased partner be expected to wait for your arrival? (Though presumably, in eternity, the whole concept of *waiting* evaporates?) If you have been married several times, do all the marriages still count? Some more than others?

a tangle with pizza crusts and used condoms, the Brazilians steal them. And now the Swedes in the next room have switched channel: bedsprings, gasps, moans, the headboard beating hard against the party wall, a cartoon noise.

■ Monsier Bombet wears a beret both indoors and out. That his complexion is unnaturally pale is because he spends most of his life in darkness. That he doesn't respond when you ask if you can have one of his biscuits is not because he is deaf – his ear must be as good as a dog's, to decipher the often mumbled and heavily accented dialogue of *noir*-ish films. What he does is this: whenever a new film opens at his local multiplex he goes to a matinee screening with a notebook, thermos and packet of biscuits, disentangles the knots of bluff and double and triple bluff in which the narrative is tied up, and writes up his verdict on the film's basic plausibility for the local newspaper.° There's a scale, the Bombet scale, ranging from 10 for utter tosh

---

° For those who are hard of hearing or for whom the plot is just too silly to bother keeping track of, there remain simply *the bits where*. The bit where he falls off his horse and into the mud. The bit where his lover has locked him in the cellar and slips on the ladder. The bit where he falls into the fire. The bit on the retreat from Moscow when he takes shelter in a ruined house where the holes in the walls are stopped up with frozen bodies. Not the bit where he sees her across the room and you know, even before he does, that it's

to 1 for minor improbability, such as guns running out of ammunition when it's the lead actor who's under fire; or blissful fluent sex between a he and a she who have only just met, simultaneous orgasms and no faffing around with condoms.

Admirable M. Bombet, but doesn't he have anything else to do? The man selling popcorn has argued that M. Bombet's notion of realism is no less a bourgeois social construct than that of the art he's criticising.° I prefer M. Bombet on those TV programmes in which 'experts' pronounce on topical social or political issues. *Contains tautology and scenes of periodic blindness, wishful thinking and smug satisfaction.*

---

all going to end badly, not that bit. The bit where the subtitles go out-of-sync, they're obviously not translating what's being said in the dialogue, it's a Friday afternoon and they've opened a few beers and you think, maybe no one else but you and the subtitlers has ever watched this film before. And even *they* gave up. The bit where she just ignores what he's said – I think I'll remember that for the rest of my life.* The bit where he falls off his horse again. And *again*.**

* A looping video clip, a vine: Beyle advancing, Mathilde retreating, a single movement on repeat.

** When, in the army, Beyle first mounted a horse, it bolted and he had to be rescued. Riding in the Bois de Boulogne, Julien in *Le Rouge et le Noir* attempts to avoid a carriage and is thrown to the ground. Riding in military formation in front of a woman he wants to impress, Lucien in *Lucien Leuwen* tumbles into the mud.

° The screenwriter Jean-Claude Carrière, recalling the early years of film, tells of French colonial administrators showing films in North

■ The lobby of the Aramis: behind the reception desk, a board with keys hanging from numbered hooks (most of the keys will open any room). A vending machine with crisps and bottled water and cans of Fanta, Coke and San Pellegrino. A TV fixed high on the wall that shows football, ice hockey, game shows and rolling news (Beyle keeps glancing at the screen: he's not interested in sport but it's only polite to know who's winning). A framed print of that photograph of steelworkers sitting out on a girder high above the streets of Manhattan, flat caps and cigarettes. A table that wobbles, two chairs. A table-football table. Another narrow table on which stands a rack of flyers for restaurants and theme parks (Franco is constantly fiddling with the flyers – neatening up, rearranging – or flicking through the Dan Browns and Harry Potters and the comics and detective novels in several languages that have accumulated on top of the vending machine). Also on that narrow table: a desktop aquarium with three gloomy fish, and often someone's glasses or a single glove. A leatherette sofa on which M's son thumbs his iPhone, then leaves.

Africa: 'A sheet was stretched between posts, the mysterious device was carefully set up, and suddenly, out in the dry night of the African bush, moving pictures appeared.' Some of the guests, either sleepy or having in mind an Islamic prohibition on the representation of the human figure, kept their eyes closed thoughout the performance. They were both there and not there. In this, they were at one with the characters in the films, and the actors playing them.

Franco: he has stubby hair and a matted beard and wears boots with complicated laces, like a man who sells organic cheese. Each day Franco stretches history a little further, making up new stories for the tourists, because the job would be intolerable if he had to tell the exact same stories every day, rain or shine; and the more he elaborates, the more ghosts and beheadings and tortures he makes up, the more generous the tourists are with their tips.°

There is also a roof terrace with a few scraggly plants in pots where on hot days the girls from the café have been known to drag out a mattress and sunbathe in the nude.

■ The body of a woman (X) at the foot of the cliffs, a body maimed by whatever it snagged against as it fell, a body the local newpaper will describe as *partially clothed*, and a London businessman (Y) shot at his holiday home – reluctantly, D.I. Aubertin phones the bank manager to cancel their round of golf. The two incidents are connected – in this genre they can't not be – and, on cue, the husband of

---

° As a babysitter he'd be useless. The child has a favourite story which she wants to hear night after night after night, and if he varies any detail – the princess has green eyes not blue, or the flying carpet has to stop for refuelling – the child screams and he has to default to the factory settings. Surely if the conjuror were to pull from the hat not a rabbit, not a dove, but a fish or a bag of walnuts . . . But no, the child insists on a rabbit.

the postmistress, who has an obsessive interest in the share dealings of Y's company, identifies the dead woman as the French wife of one of Y's business rivals. Y's laptop, mobile phone and car are missing. A local mechanic who recently worked on Y's car claims he was never paid. The mechanic's son is known to the local police as a low-level drug-dealer. The business rival, arriving on the midday train, says that he knew his wife was having an affair with Y but believes this ended several months ago.

So far, thinks Aubertin, glancing through the tourist brochures in the lobby of the Red Lion, where the business rival and his companion – and who is *she*? – are checking in, this is shaping up to be a routine Sunday-evening TV drama: infidelity, seagulls, rent-a-line dialogue, ads in the breaks for panty liners and macho cars. Aubertin himself drives a six-year-old VW Golf. He is not married and doesn't have a dog. He did but it died. No one has ever described him as *craggy*. He speaks French but that's not much use now, given that the French woman is dead. He'd like to be played by Robert De Niro, but he knows that the budget won't stretch even to Robson Green.

After the Red Lion, Aubertin is going to visit the woman who cleans Y's house and stocks the fridge when she knows that Y is coming down. It was pretty stupid of Y to bring X to a place where both he and his wife are familiar to the locals – if that's what he did do – but people *are* stupid, a fact which can make a mockery of all attempts to establish any rational motivation. Stupidity is the wild card.

The daughter of the woman who stocks the fridge is the girlfriend of the mechanic's son. The postmistress is blackmailing the secretary of the golf club over his affair with the vicar's wife. The issue of overpriced second homes standing empty for much of the year while the locals can't afford an unheated shed is irrelevant but may trigger some useful publicity.

Back at the station, the whiteboard in the incident room shows a scribble of arrows and dotted lines, and Aubertin's head is aching. He has a stomach-ache too and feels as if he is going to be sick at any moment. He suspects that he's caught a bug from something rotten in the genre itself, something long past its use-by date, a plate of leftover subplots at the back of the fridge that are growing mould. They should be sent to the lab for analysis, but it's a bit late for that. When Aubertin arrives at the cottage of the woman who cleans Y's house the first question he asks, and urgently, is can he use her toilet? She tells him up the stairs and first left, and while he is reaching for the loo roll he notices two books that have fallen behind the radiator. One of them is an anthology of *Daily Telegraph* obituaries. The other is a thriller; set in a picturesque coastal town, its plot involves not two murders but three, and Aubertin thinks he might as well just sit tight and wait for Z.°

° Another thriller is found behind a radiator in Georges Perec's *53 Days*, whose title alludes to the time it took Beyle to write *La Chartreuse de Parme*. At the time Perec died he had written just eleven

■ The hard roll of the ball, then the rapid-fire staccato of the rotating bars and the stiff little figures. The clack of the ball through the goal and hitting the base. This table-football game is a breakthrough. The boy is M's son. He is eleven years old. Beyle – who suspects that the boy is earning pocket money by working for the police as an informer and that what he's tapping out on his phone is his daily report to his controller° – asks him how his mother is. The boy shrugs. And his sister? The boy pretends not to hear. He is playing like a pro, his hands flicking between the handles as if he's conducting a precision bombing raid.

On the TV on the wall, forest fires, then ice hockey.

Beyle is too slow, too clumsy, and loses every game. Eventually the boy leaves, bored by Beyle's incompetence. Franco, fiddling with the tourist brochures, laughs. Beyle feels that he has let the boy down, but can't see that getting better at table football will remedy anything.

Meanwhile, the bad news is that while unblocking the toilet on the third floor the plumber has discovered that the

---

chapters. Beyle haunts the book: several of his pseudonyms are used as the names of incidental characters; there's a 'Professor Shetland'; and the notes for the unwritten chapters offer Grenoble, the Chartreuse massif, names of Paris streets that Beyle lived in, a chestnut tree and 'l'acheteuse du Parme'.

° The controller has a photo of his grandchildren on his desk and just two more years to stay out of trouble before his pension kicks in. He is not a *bad* person.

bowl has been leaking and water has seeped under the floor tiles, which need taking up and re-laying. Did no one notice the smell? Well, now that you mention it. Haven't there been any complaints? Or is this how toilets in cheap hotels are supposed to smell? The good news is that because another job has been cancelled, the plumber can start tomorrow.

■ In the drawer of his dressing table: phone charger, packet of paracetamol, knife to sharpen goose quills, an AA battery, a boiled sweet. Beyle could swear his passport was there too when he last looked, but he can't remember when he did last look. It's not there now. Someone else (a blond German?) is walking around being him. He wishes them good luck. He should contact the local consulate, but they'll ask him for proof of who he is and things will get tricky.

A fly – a large one, bloated with frustration – buzzes against the window. Beyle opens the window to let it out. His passport has changed into a fly.°

° There are *edges*. The signs that you are approaching one of the world's edges might include, for example, not just one but all the neon lights in the pool room flickering. A sound like the sound of rigging clacking against the metal masts of many hundreds of boats in a marina. Rapturous applause after an opera by Cimarosa, relayed over a crackly radio. The beep-beep noise made by a reversing truck. The sound of a reel of film spinning loose, the end flapping free. Or, while you are cutting wood outside your cabin in the forest, a

■ Another thing that dying may be like (Anna's suggestion): when the train you are riding in comes to a stop but your body is still moving forward, that tiny backwards jolt, into yourself. *La petite mort.*

Another thing the afterlife is like: writer's block.

■ *Ecrivain*, it doesn't say in Beyle's missing passport.° Thinking of books he knows he's not going to get around to writing, he starts to write reviews of them instead, as if they *had been written*. The reviews are exemplary: praise where praise is due but severe on plots he considers ridiculous, arguments faulty, style slapdash. The reviews will be printed

---

sudden noise behind you – the crack of a twig on the path, a rustle among the branches – and you turn to see the bob-tail of a deer bouncing away, or nothing at all, and when you turn back there is equally nothing: no pile of logs, no jacket discarded over by the pickup, no pickup, no cabin, no forest, just the axe or the chainsaw in your hands.

° He was never a professional writer. He was, at various times, a clerk in the War Office and in a grocery shop, a soldier, a travelling salesman and a consul. He spent a *lot* of time on horseback or in stage coaches. But still, a writer of sorts: a man sitting at a desk in a room, preferably on the fourth floor.•

• The fourth floor was important. *Le Rouge et le Noir*: "I'm looking for solitude and rural tranquillity in the only place they exist in France, on the fourth floor overlooking the Champs-Élysées." Beyle

in literary journals. Sometimes the editors will forward letters from authors who have taken offence.

He presses 'print' and nothing happens. He quits Word, re-opens, tries again, nothing. He unplugs the cable at both ends and plugs it back in. He stares at the printer and counts slowly to ten. He restarts. He opens and closes trays and flaps, he presses buttons, he looks for the re-set button which will need a paperclip to get to it and he doesn't have any, or he does but finding one will be pure luck. He's rattled, and he rattles the whole machine with a vengeance. It is made not to last. The grey plastic will yield to only so much pressure before it snaps without warning and no guarantee will cover it.

Maybe he should call it a day; on the other hand, maybe he should buy a new printer. He opens Google, then blinks back at the cursor blinking in the search box, having forgotten what he's searching for. 'Robust' is an overused word.

---

in a letter, 1834, after noting that "not a single dreary English family visiting Rome but reads the *Promenades*": "How happy I would be on a fourth storey, writing another such book, if I had bread!" The higher the floor, the cheaper the rent. "In Paris servants live at the top of the house. True love rarely descends below the fifth floor, and then sometimes it jumps out the window." Beyle wrote *La Chartreuse de Parme* in 1838 at 8 rue Caumartin, Paris, on the fourth floor.

■ That place behind the high brick wall with razor wire running along the top – is it what Beyle thinks it is?

It is, says his driving instructor, a boy of around sixteeen with the patience of ten saints. His older brother is inside, doing time for false imprisonment.

Beyle stalls the engine in the middle of the street, perpendicular to the traffic, while attempting a three-point turn. He glances at the dashboard and then away: too much information. He's thinking of the instructor's brother, serving out his sentence before he's prodded back onto the streets on a rainy Thursday, when he catches sight of M on the pavement – and then she's gone again, through the visitors' gate and into the prison with a file or a hacksaw hidden inside a cake for her lover.°

It was a mistake to have moved on to the three-point turn before having mastered the clutch.°° The instructor

---

° Prisons in Beyle's novels were more stage sets for operas than Wormwood Scrubs. Julien entering the prison in Besançon in *Le Rouge et le Noir*: "He judged the architecture to be of the early fourteenth century; he admired its grace and pointed lightness. Through a narrow gap between two walls on the far side of a deep court he could glimpse a wonderful view." The view from the Farnese Tower in which Fabrizio is imprisoned in *La Chartreuse* is also fine, encompassing much of northern Italy; it's in this prison that Fabrizio discovers his freedom.

°° In Elizabeth Bowen's *To the North* (1932), Emmeline and Markie borrow a cottage in the country for a weekend. It's a fiasco. Markie,

puts a chilly hand over Beyle's on the gear stick and helps him get the car into reverse. This really isn't working.

■ Beyle indoors, staying out of the wind, or under house arrest for opinions deemed prejudicial to the government.

Beyle noticing a bruise, yellowing, on his elbow, and having no memory of what caused it. Beyle listening to the Swedish couple in the next room shouting or fucking, always one or the other, do they never sleep? He'll miss them when they've gone.

Beyle appalled by the black glass façade of the Banco Popolare di Milano (but the dismay will wear off).

Beyle concocting a fantasy in which M's children are kidnapped by bandits and she is in need of comfort and tenderness. Beyle trying, desperately, to remember the children's names.

Beyle calling M, but she never picks up. And when she does, he stammers, or rattles on like an idiot.

---

bored, plucks Beyle's *De l'Amour* from a shelf and reads aloud several paragraphs before concluding: 'Rot.' Why is it rot? Emmeline asks. Because 'One's got no time for all that.' Emmeline, attempting to rescue Beyle, offers masculine achievement: in the army, Beyle crossed the Alps on horseback. Oh, says Markie, no doubt '*he* could have driven a car'. (Markie doesn't drive: 'because machinery bored him; also on the principle that it is a mistake to do anything anyone else can do for one'.)

Beyle unplugging the bedside light and placing his hand over the socket, curious to know what leaking electricity feels like and disappointed when he feels nothing.

Beyle drinking too much and seeing M with the sunglasses-seller in the alley behind the Irish pub. Beyle drinking too little and seeing M watching over her daughter sleeping. Beyle not putting any of this into writing because it reeks of sentiment.

Late at night, Beyle writing a letter to M instead and then, in the morning, tearing it up.

Beyle falling asleep at odd times of the day. Beyle checking his spam folder. Beyle stumbling on the stairs, falling headlong and wondering if he's broken anything.

Beyle sober as a ("I've forgotten the term of comparison"), heroically confronting the kidnappers and making them, despite their guns, see reason. Beyle refusing to answer the questions asked by the reporters camped out on his doorstep, insisting on his right to privacy.

Beyle being rebuked by a woman in the shopping mall for staring at her breasts (no, no, he was just trying to read the slogan on her T-shirt).

Beyle, while scratching a mosquito bite on his ankle, remembering that it is always better to be in love than not in love – even if there is no chance, *ever*, of that love being reciprocated.°

° "When one has passions, one is never bored; without them, one is stupid."

Beyle with a torch on the roof of the Aramis flashing messages in code to a woman on a planet that has ceased to exist.

Beyle finding in a charity shop an English translation of a novel he hasn't yet written and that looks, except for a pencil underlining of a single innocuous phrase on page 12, unread.

Beyle regretting having chucked his SS overcoat into a bin, because the evenings here can be chilly.

Beyle remembering that 'overcoat' was once a slang word for condom.

Beyle reading to the end of a paragraph and then wondering how he got there, he must have drifted off, and having to re-read the whole paragraph to establish exactly where he lost the thread.

Beyle sitting on a swing in a children's playground in light drizzle, observing a woman's shoe on the asphalt and thinking how irredeemably *dull* this town is.°

° Rilke: 'You must have seen them: these small towns and tiny villages of my homeland. They have learned one day by heart and they scream it out into the sunlight over and over again like great grey parrots. Near night though they grow preternaturally pensive. You can see it in the town squares, where they struggle to solve the dark question that hangs in the air. It is touching, and a little ludicrous, to the foreigner, because he knows without a second thought that if there is an answer – any answer at all – it certainly won't come from the small towns and villages of my homeland, try as sincerely as they might, poor things.'

Beyle booking a flight to get out of here and turning up at the airport and getting as far as passport control and being refused permission to fly: he's stateless, no other place will accept him, even as a refugee.

■ Signing in as a visitor at the fitness centre, Beyle is required to fill in a form. Does he have chest pains brought on by physical activity? Yes/no. Has he ever lost consciousness or fallen over as a result of dizzyness? Yes/no. Does he have a heart condition?°

In the spirit of St Peter, he lies three times.

He sits for a hour in the sauna, sweating out the brandy he has drunk in the deceased-writers' club and the humiliation of rejection by M and of spending the last years of his life in a dull job in the dull town of Civitavecchia ("I might as well be in Borneo"), and when he comes back into the changing room he walks into a kerfuffle over a pigeon which, having found its way in, cannot find a way out. It flies into a mirror and falls to the ground.

When he walks out into the street, Beyle feels giddy and has to lean against a wall.°° This is where M's daughter finds

---

° "Whenever anyone speaks to me of you, I feel that I am transparent." – Beyle to Dembowski, 30 June 1819.

°° Beyle was forty-three when, having run out of excuses, he got around to writing his novels. He had sixteen years left. During much

him, panting like a dog on a hot day, and a chair appears by magic and she sits him down and brings him water and tells him her dreams.

■ At fifteen, aware that she's being looked at by boys, M's daughter walks like an ingénue model on a catwalk who's about to trip over. Looked at by men too, Beyle among them. He has some old-world thing going on with her mother. He has some other thing going on with the sunglasses-seller outside the station, the one called John, the one from whom she buys a pair of fake Ray-Bans. He smiles as he takes her money and asks if she'd care for anything else and she smiles back and says no and walks away and half a minute later half changes her mind but she doesn't go back. Maybe next time.°

---

of that period he was ill: migraines, tremors, swellings, losses of memory and of speech, pains in his testicles and elsewhere. His ailments were caused not so much by the STD, perhaps syphilis, that he picked up while still a teenager as by the treatments prescribed for this. As an amputee may sense a phantom limb, in his afterlife Beyle still feels the pains and humiliations of his actual life; it's what makes an afterlife imaginable.

° In Ryu Murakami's *Almost Transparent Blue* (1977), Lilly picks up *La Chartreuse de Parme* from the bedside table and starts reading 'with a peaceful absentminded expression'. '"You sure read at weird times, silly Lilly," I said, picking up the syringe that had fallen from the shelf and rolled along the floor.'

She puts on the sunglasses, though the sky is cloudy.°

■ The turn of a head, a hand brushing hair from a brow, a profile in shadow – and when the head turns again and it is not M, it's no one even resembling M, Beyle's heart is left spinning like an upturned bicycle wheel. It is as if, he thinks, they *have been* married: have been married for so long that they've come out on the other side, past the scrap yards and into the hinterland, completing each other's sentences, slotting into each other like pieces of Lego. In bed, one of them puts their book down and turns onto their side, the other switches the light out.

Another person Beyle could swear he's seen is the Marquis de la Mole, poking around, *squidging*, among the shellfish at the fish market. Here, queueing at a supermarket till with a basket of beans and breakfast cereals, is a man who looks exactly like what Beyle imagines Voltaire looked like.

° Not Ray-Bans but Balthus. Every street has in it a man carrying a plank of wood (or sometimes a ladder) and a child getting under everyone's feet and a man who fancies himself as Napoleon and a woman stepping into or out of the gutter and another woman carrying a middle-aged baby and a cook stopped dead in his tracks by a flashback to how he behaved last night and a fifteen-year-old girl being molested. Round the corner, she has learned, there's more likely to be a drunk urinating against a wall than a friendly policeman, but just possibly a boy with a fierce grin who can talk about Aristotle.

Perhaps it *is* Voltaire? There, standing in line at a cashpoint, is M. Daru.° There is Angelique, reading *Hello!* magazine in a café. Bonjour, Angelique. There, doing t'ai chi exercises in the park, is someone whose name he can't recall, someone from the Russian campaign, someone in a carriage from someplace to another, some regular at the Caffè Greco in the Via Condotti. He hopes he doesn't run into his father: he's still far from ready for the peace that passeth all understanding. He wouldn't mind bumping into Edward Edwards.°°

■ M is aware of Beyle's presence too, in the town, but he is not *following* her, even though it might look like he is, to her. 'He reads my letters, my bills . . .'

Often, Beyle has the sensation that *he* is being followed. That woman who is looking into the window of a shoe shop, for example – as he passes, she turns, and he can feel her staring after him and he's convinced he has seen her

---

° Who generously took Beyle under his wing and got him his first job in Paris, as a clerk at the War Office; the man for whom Beyle was always a disappointment, and whose wife Beyle tried to sleep with; the man who, late in the day, tried to buy one of Beyle's books and was outraged by the price: "Thirty francs? Is it possible! That infant – ignorant as a carp!"

°° An Englishman: "the only member of his race who was accustomed to promoting gaiety".

before. Most likely he's mistaken but still, he avoids badly lit alleyways at night. He assumes that one of the African sellers of sunglasses and wooden statuettes outside the station is under instruction from M to kill him, and hopes she hasn't settled for the lowest bidder. He would want this person – almost certainly a man, even though every one of the women he has known has been more sane, organised and determined, or at least one of the three, than any man – he would want this person to be good at what he does, clean and efficient and quick, not a nervous first-timer. No one would want this bungled, no one likes seeing anyone crumpled but still alive in the gutter, astonished by the colour of his own blood.

John, he hopes; he'd trust John. If that really is his name. How much she's paid him up-front, how much to come later, is up to her. One reason he loves M is that she doesn't stint.

■ The sensation, but magnified, that you experience when climbing a staircase of twelve steps and your feet, or one of them, believes that there is a thirteenth; or the sensation of being closely embraced without there being anyone doing the embracing.

■ Come, the plumber gestures. The toilet must have been leaking for some time, because the water – and, yes, the

urine and and whatever else gets deposited in a toilet bowl
– has seeped not just under the floor tiles but down through
the floor and into the shower room below, where the tiles
are coming away from the wall.

So Beyle follows him up the stairs – with the plumber's
mate, the squeaky teenager, close behind: he is being kidnapped – along the corridor and into the shower room on
the second floor. The plumber is large and heavy and grey
and it bears repeating, it's a wonder how he could ever fit
under a sink. He taps a tile in the shower with his knuckles,
then looks at Beyle and gestures for him to do the same.
Beyle taps, half-expecting someone in the next room to tap
back – they could devise a code, a language made up entirely of taps in which they could tell each other jokes and
plot their escape.

Then the plumber taps a tile on the opposite wall, by the
door, and so does Beyle: a different, more rounded sound.
The plumber nods, satisfied.

Down the corridor, a woman wearing nothing but a yellow towel is waiting for them to vacate the shower room.
Beyle understands that the plumber has pitched a tent in
his life and will be here for some time.

■ A sunshine day, at last. The café has closed early, a notice in the window announcing 'family bereavement', and
Beyle, Franco and the two girls are driving to a lake an hour
out of town in a rented car. Franco is driving; tall girl will

drive on the way back. Tall girl° is rangy and loose-limbed; for the car, the 'economy' option, she has had to fold herself in. Anna is dark-haired and a little plump.

'What are you looking at?' Anna asks.

He likes the shape of her breasts and the shapes of the fields they are driving past and how the trees stick together for safety.

Now they are sitting on plastic chairs around a plastic table on a café terrace and listening to plastic music. Beyle is wearing shorts and is feeling conspicuously pale and wondering why he agreed to this outing and he has a headache too, from sitting too long in the sun without a hat. Franco, baggy swimming trunks. Tall girl, bikini. Anna is wearing a polka-dot dress. Beyle fishes an insect out of his beer and examines it, squirming, on his finger.

They are talking about Anna's mother-in-law in the care home and the ignominy of getting old and the consolations of religion. The silver crucifix around Anna's neck is riding at a slant above her breasts. Tall girl and Franco are having none of it: no happy-ever-after, nor ever was or will be. Anna becomes animated and declares that believers are not children who have signed up to a fairy tale with a guaranteed happy ending. Far from it. It's *non*-believers who are taking the easy option: they can act as they want, follow any whim,

---

° If I give her a name I will need to make eye contact, take some responsibility.

without consequences. In contrast, a girl like herself lives with the terror of judgement, knowing that if she behaves in certain ways she will be condemning herself to an eternity of hellfire, and while she is saying this Beyle is watching a bead of sweat trickling down from between her collar bones, stalling at the crucifix, finding a way down.

■ Looking at a painting in the town gallery, no Old Master, Beyle has a feeling of déjà vu, even though the painting didn't exist until a century after he died. A trick of the light? A false memory? He steps forward. The attendant slumped in a chair by the door wakes up and raises his gun.

It's a painting of the afterlife: no shadows.

More paintings, glorious ones, in the afternoon screening of *The Stendhal Syndrome*.° Beyle likes the girl, who is called Anna, though that she's young, pretty and in charge of the investigation of a serial killer can only mean that horrible things are going to happen to her. He likes the paintings too and he likes the big fish that kisses Anna after she's fainted in the Uffizi, a fish-kiss.°°

Scribble scribble – that's M. Bombet in the row in front, busily recording the implausibilities. Digestives still

---

° 1996; director, Dario Argento.

°° Beyle's own description of being overwhelmed by art, of being barely able to stand upright, included no fish, but you can't control

70

wrapped, no time even to pour coffee from his thermos, he can't keep up.

Meanwhile, it's warm, the seats are comfortable, and Beyle nods off. He misses the first rape and most of the blood and gore and when he wakes up Anna is wearing a blonde wig and in love with a Frenchman called Marie Beyle, at first chastely and then less so. A scene in a garden, an idyll. Anonymous phone calls. Marie gets killed in a room of classical sculptures. Anna's therapist turns murderous. Then Anna kills her former lover by slamming a car boot down on his neck and is carried off to an asylum. The end credits roll.

The light, when Beyle exits the cinema, is startlingly bright, as if *this* is the film set. He blinks. He sees a child falling while running and scraping a knee and not feeling any pain until its parents bristle with concern and *then* the child starts bawling.

■ The sky all blue, just a single wispy cloud hung out to dry. Beyle is lying on his back in the lake. The water is cold. The cloud starts to separate, an edge trailing off like a monkey's tail.

---

these things. You write and you post what you've written through a sort of letter box to your readers – but it is not a letter box, it is a shredding machine. Various people attempt to piece the pieces back together. Some of them are even paid for this.

He turns over in the water, and looking back to the shore sees Anna sitting by an upturned boat. Behind her, Franco and the tall girl are walking into the trees that border the narrow beach. There is no one else around.

He doggy-paddles towards the beach. When the water becomes too shallow for swimming, he has to stand. The stones are slippery: he walks with the awkwardness of a child who is just learning how to put one foot in front of the other, flailing his arms to stay balanced, and his ankle turns and he stumbles.

Anna walks towards him, grinning, telling him he looks like an albatross. Neither of them has ever seen an albatross. He wonders why he has not noticed her freckles before: maybe they only appear on sunny days. For a man with aspirations to be a writer he has been criminally un-observant.

Anna ducks under his arm and takes some of his weight, though she is barefoot herself. Beside the upturned boat she has made a sort of nest of their towels and bags. When they reach the boat and Beyle leans on it to take the weight off his feet, they kiss.

He is overcome by clumsiness, *literariness*, and although Anna is more than kind the beach is pebbly, his ankle hurts, and the whole episode is what Beyle when writing his book on love termed a *fiasco*.°

° The Beyle who, when visiting a seventeen-year-old courtesan in 1821 ("She was adorable, I perhaps had never seen anyone prettier"),

■ Facts? What *facts?* The tour company that employs Franco as a guide has received a complaint about his elaboration of history and has told him to 'stick to the facts'.

Franco kicks the vending machine so hard that *Teach Yourself Astrology* teeters on the edge, overbalances and thuds to the floor. Besides, no one has to *believe* what he tells them. Some people believe that the Earth is rotating at 1,000 miles per hour and orbiting the sun at 67,000 miles per hour and speeding along with neighbouring galaxies towards god-knows-where, others that the Earth was created in six days or from a single drop of milk. No need to take a hard line. The Earth is both round (we've been to the planetarium) and flat (which is how we experience it), and we can cope with this. If children can both know that Father Christmas doesn't exist and also expect him to deliver, and on time, why not adults?

Besides, even if the Earth is flat it's not *flat* flat. There are folds, as in a dress that is lying flat on the bed. Anna takes up the dress and steps into it. It's lovely, Beyle says. Not too short at all. And then she *mmm*s with her lips and takes off the perfect dress and chooses another from a row of hangers – also flat, like a painting on a wall – and steps into that one. Repeat. Repeat. All this putting on and taking

---

after his rejection by Mathilde, "failed entirely", had to resort to a "manual expedient" (*ce jeu du main*), and then, after his place was taken by a friend, had to listen to gales of laughter from the girl's room.

off: Beyle thinks they should stay in. But she really does want to go out.

He could check the time but instead he goes to the window and watches people walking by in the street and notes how rarely their lives fit them: they're too baggy, too tight under the armpits, they belong to someone slightly else.

■ Count Corner at the battle of Borodino, 1812, outside Moscow, 70,000 casualties in a single day: "Is this damn battle never going to finish?" Napoleon had a bad cold on that day; he stayed in his tent, feeling wretched, and fluffed his chances of forcing a victory. Beyle too has a cold, probably caught during the retreat from Moscow in sub-zero temperatures.° He is shivering in an unheated rehearsal studio under a railway arch with a group of actors and he's lost count of the number of times they've run through the scene in which he has to fall from his chair to the floor. The chair is meant to represent a seat in a train; Beyle thinks of it more as a horse. He has to fall in a way that looks natural, that doesn't obscure the other actors, that establishes the fact that it's unlikely he'll have any more lines, and that doesn't look unintentionally comic. He has to act dying. The female actor sitting next to him then has to give a little

---

° Beyle to his sister, 7 December 1812: "I have lost everything and have only the clothes on my back. What is much nicer is the fact that I'm now thin."

shriek of alarm or surprise, preferably both, a lot harder than any scripted line. Beyle recalls the standard advice on how to act drunk – act sober, because that is what drunk people do – and gets confused: act *not* dying? Fall sideways, fall forward? More of a *crumple*, maybe? He has bruises on his elbows and shins. The director still isn't happy. Take it again from 'Do you remember?' Beyle stifles a sneeze. Fall. Fall again. Fall better.

■ World domination was no longer an option. Napoleon grew fat, and eventually he withdrew with a flea-ridden dog to the small park behind the bus station, where he spends his days among the recycling bins quarrelling with a band of other fallen emperors and shabby ex-generals over who to blame for their defeats. Talk to him and he'll tell you a sad tale about how he found his dog licking the face of its dead master on a moonlit battlefield.° Which battlefield? you ask, and he shrugs: all battlefields are the same, aren't they? The stench, the mud, the corpses robbed of their boots.

He boasts, too, about how he planned his seductions of women like military campaigns – here a feint, there a rapid advance – and though many were successful he is still obsessed by the one who got away, a woman who had built

---

° True story: 1796, a battle against the Austrians. On St Helena, Napoleon had a dog named Sambo which had its ears cut off and looked like a seal.

around herself a sort of Maginot Line, except this one left no loophole for invasion. If she'd been saving herself for God, which she wasn't, the Catholic Church would have claimed her as a saint, and there'd be shrines and an annual public holiday. Irresistible force, immovable object. No wonder he looks exhausted.

He tosses an empty in the general direction of the litter bin and misses by a mile. His speech is slurred. There are scabs on his forehead, flies buzzing, and he asks you for a cigarette and you look into his watery eyes. This is not Napoleon, for sure.° But nor is it Beyle.

■ Late afternoon. Beyle is jogging in the park. His running shoes have fluorescent orange flashes, the only colour they had in his size. On his headphones he is listening to a Scandinavian band that Franco has enthused about, but they are so bad that Beyle can only think that Franco is playing a joke on him. He pockets the headphones.

Now he can hear traffic, birdsong, someone playing

° '"Delusions of grandeur", of which believing oneself to be Napoleon became the archetype, rose to extraordinary medical and cultural prominence during the July Monarchy. By 1840 it accounted for a quarter of all diagnoses of insanity.' – Mike Jay, *London Review of Books*, 21 May 2015. Ben Sonnenberg in *Lost Property* (1991) quotes a man who in the 1890s remembered seeing Napoleon in Moscow: 'He was very tall and had a long white beard.'

drums, children shouting, dogs barking. There are many dogs, and most belong to single women. One of the women is accompanied by five dogs: a professional dog-walker, Beyle assumes, with an hourly rate.

As he pounds along, he sees ahead of him a black dog with the kind of short curly hair that properly belongs to a much smaller dog, and when he passes a bench on which a woman and a young boy are seated the dog barks and runs after him. Why isn't the dog on a lead, why isn't the woman calling the dog to heel? – but right now Beyle is not looking back, he is trying to run faster, though even if he were fitter he'd never be able to outpace this dog.

Something bad is about to happen, and then that something does happen: the dog bites him on the back of his leg, between calf and ankle, *ouch*. Beyle stumbles to the side of the path and sits on the grass. The woman is shouting at him, furious: it is all his own fault, he aggravated the dog by running too close, and then something about his being a *man*. The dog is still barking, enjoying this game. Beyle looks down: it's more nip than bite, but there's a spot or two of blood on his white socks. Rabies, he thinks: acute inflammation of the brain, followed by excruciating death. He feels suddenly very thirsty, or as if he's about to vomit. Franco's Scandinavian band has put a curse on him for not liking their music.

He recognises the boy standing next to the shouting woman as M's son, so the woman is probably M's sister, though she doesn't look like M at all. On the other hand, in her outrage at his being a man, there's a resemblance. The boy is looking at him – curious, puzzled, complicit. Has he never seen a nineteenth-century French novelist before? Or just not one who's been bitten by a dog?

Somewhere not far off the drumming noise continues, uninterrupted, and then birdsong too and the siren of a police car or ambulance in traffic, almost bucolic.

■ If John is really going to kill me, Beyle thinks,° walking past a Starbucks, stepping out of the way of a blind man coming towards him with a flailing white stick – *tap tap tap*, another dotted line – it will probably be in the morning, when he's fully awake and alert, a time that is good for clean killing. Or it will be in the late afternoon, after John has

---

° "When thoughts come to me in the middle of the street, I am always on the verge of colliding with a passer-by, falling or being run over by the carriages. One day in Paris near the Rue d'Amboise (one occasion out of a hundred), I stared at Doctor Edwards• without recognising him. That is, there were two actions; the first said right enough: 'There's Doctor Edwards', but the second was busy thinking, and failed to add: 'You must say hello to him and speak to him.'"

• Edwards – brother of Edward Edwards – was an English doctor in Paris who had a passion for dissecting frogs in order to discover a cure for women's chest ailments: "You know that each year in Paris eleven hundred young women die from the cold they catch coming out of balls. I've seen the official statistics."

had a nap and taken a shower and shaved, and he is relaxed and calm and has chosen his clothes with care – not that he has much choice over what to wear, this John, but in the movies everyone lives in fancier apartments and has 'wardrobe assistants', everything is more *glossy*, which is what people expect of the afterlife too.

■ And if Beyle were to die – Franco during one of their chess games, suggesting thereby a sequel, an Afterlife 2.

Black knight d4 to f5.

Beyle sees a forest fire raging on the TV screen.

The Swedish couple walk through the lobby, her hand already inside his jeans. From the desk with the tourist brochures, a glove falls to the floor.

Did Beyle ever fight a duel?

He'd rather not talk about that.°

Franco once played Laertes in a production of *Hamlet*.

° His first duel, fought in his late teens, was a muddled, anticlimactic affair. He suspected that the seconds hadn't loaded the pistols. It left him feeling confused and angry, not at all like his heroes in literature.•

• Beyle to his sister Pauline, backtracking on his reading lists: "those damned books I mentioned just now: you might as well try to work out what a windmill looks like on the basis of a plough. The truth is just the opposite of what they say, it's as simple as that. If they showed the world as it is, they'd fill people with horror."

For six nights a week plus two matinees, he fought the duel with Hamlet with a poisoned sword, died and was resurrected and went to the pub and then to bed – and he, not Hamlet, was sleeping with Ophelia, from the day of the first read-through – and came back the next day and did it all over again. It was fun, he says, capturing Beyle's last bishop.

Next, crowds of people, uncountable, at a border crossing between one life and another. Next, market expectations in the retail sector.

Why, Anna asks, if Beyle is so good at maths, which he claims to be,° does he always lose to Franco at chess?

° Maths – which kept at bay "hypocrisy and vagueness, my two pet aversions" – was Beyle's route out of the provinces: he won a prize that enabled him to study in Paris. The bedroom in which his mother died when he was aged seven (his mother whom he loved: "I wanted to cover my mother with kisses and for there not to be any clothes") was kept locked for ten years by his father (whom he hated: "gloomy, timorous, rancorous, unfriendly"), but Beyle was given a key and allowed into the room "to work at my mathematics". He let his hair grow wild, "so much did I begrudge the half-hour I would have had to waste in getting it cut". He remained puzzled by the law that a minus times a minus equals a plus: if so, surely you should be able, by multiplying one of your debts by another, to make a fortune? As Beyle and his father waited together for the carriage that would take him to the capital after winning that prize, his father wept: "The only impression his tears made on me was to find him ugly," Beyle later wrote. Paris was a disappointment: there were no mountains, and the trees were pruned.

■ Everything in the care home, Anna says, is slightly sticky. And the dog has disappeared. Poisoned by the cook, Anna says.

One down, Beyle says. He was starting to get worried. There are more dogs around than there should be, or need to be. Only this morning he watched a young dog in the park becoming excited, rushing from one tree or patch of ground to another, then back again, then on to another tree, trying to decide on exactly the right place to pee.

Is there a right place? Anna asks. It must know that it can't sniff every tree in the park.

Yes, there's a right place, Beyle says. Why else would the dog be expending so much nervous energy?

How is the dog to know until after it has chosen?

It will know, in its doggy way.

■ *I'm in the clinic. I don't know, it could be another hour at least. Love you.*

Beyle is in the waiting room, waiting for a tetanus injection for the dog bite° and listening to the audible halves of conversations on mobile phones.

Sam, you can't just spring it on them, they'll bury you.

° Of course he's not going to get rabies and die. He's here for the duration, at least of this book. But in this place where *no game is being played*, certain conventions – such as looking both ways before crossing a street – are still worth respecting.

Better safe than sorry, he's heard tell, though he's not sure about that, there must be other options available.

I've told you not to call me on this number. Yes.

If he had to choose between the woman sitting on the opposite side of the room, legs crossed, eyes closed, headphones in ears, who has been waiting even longer than he has and will be called earlier, and the Photoshopped woman in the lingerie in the magazine that's open on his knees, he would choose the woman wearing the headphones. The circumstances in which he might have to make that choice are obscure.

It's not the midfield, the midfield's not the problem, it's why he never plays two up front.

It's likely that, with her headphones plugged in, the woman won't hear her name being called and will miss her turn. He wonders what hurt she is seeking relief from, and whether two tablets swallowed three times daily after food will make any difference at all.

Oh, just buy it. You can always take it back if it doesn't fit.

Or she is not waiting *for* anything at all, she's here just to wait.

I don't think we should rush this.

A flyer pinned to the noticeboard announces 'Sexual Health Week', a year out of date. In front of the noticeboard is an empty wheelchair – someone paralysed since birth has just stood up and walked away while no one was looking.

Sometimes I wonder who I'm talking to, I really do.

In sympathy with the headphones woman, Beyle too

closes his eyes, dozes off, dreams: M and her children and her sister will be coming round soon, and he should have something – cakes from the café over the street – to offer them. Instead, he begins to fashion coat hangers out of bits of wire and scraps of wood that happen to be lying around. But he rushes it, impatient, and to fix the bits of wood together he uses carpet tacks too long for the job and a hammer that is too big, and so makes holes in the kitchen table. When M and her sister arrive, they'll think: making coat hangers, he bodges even that.

■ People who like classical music, says Anna, live in very clean houses.

The way trains slow down when they're passing through disused or abandoned stations, and then pick up speed again when they're past – it's respectful, Anna says. Beyle thinks it's slightly creepy.

Has Beyle ever slept with men? Anna asks.°

How's the spaghetti puttanesca? Anna asks.

It tastes bland, ersatz, dilute. It tastes of the afterlife.

In bed, Anna pinches Beyle, the soft part above the hip bone. For a man who's been dead so long he's wearing remarkably well.

° He might have expected to be asked about his books, yes – 'What made you become a writer?', 'Where do you get your stories?' – but not this. He hasn't *agreed* to be here at all.

You're some kind of spy, aren't you? Anna asks.°

■ M, returning after her dinner with Beyle to the apartment she is renting with her children, or returning after meeting John or posting a letter or just going for a walk – I don't have to be exact here, I'm not giving *evidence* – switches on the TV, sits on the sofa and watches a woman in a yellow bikini trying to sell her a waffle iron. Holidays are unnatural, she says aloud; they just shift you from a place where everyone is trying to sell you things to a place where they sell you different things, or the same things but they look different because the packaging is unfamiliar. *Animals don't take holidays.*

° All outsiders arouse suspicion, writers especially (scribbling away in their little notebooks, trying to make sense of things). In Paris in the 1970s many people thought that Harry Mathews was a CIA agent. In *My Life in CIA* – an 'autobiographical novel' – he relates how, given that denying any CIA involvement only confirmed the general assumption, he plays along. He starts to enjoy the practice of 'discreet conspicuousness', sets up deals to sell false information, finds his life becoming 'like a movie I'd rather watch than be in', becomes the target of a hired killer, and ends the book herding a flock of four hundred sheep down from their summer to their winter pastures.

More than a spy, Beyle is a double agent, working for both sides (France/Italy, Classicism/Romanticism, art/life), and he knows it's pointless to deny it.

'Birds do,' says her son, who is standing in the doorway, watching her.

Seasonal migration is not the same thing, it is work not holiday, but she's not going to argue the point because then they'd get into what's 'natural' and what's not. *Any* argument with her son she finds depressing.

M goes into her bedroom and lies down and closes her eyes. The woman in the bikini is filling a plastic barrel with water from a tap fixed to a wall, except now her bikini is an orange sari. Sheets hang stiffly from washing lines strung across an open yard. The building is an abandoned hospital or prison or mission school, but right now it serves as a hostel for the town's shifting population of African migrants, who drift slowly in and out of the rooms around the yard. One of them is John. She follows him through a doorway into a long, dark storage room with cardboard boxes piled high against the walls and then up a concrete stairway. She is wearing the wrong shoes for this,° and there's no railing.

° M's dreams rarely enter horror territory; they are kitchen sink, or comedy of manners. *Contains infrequent sexual references, moderate threat and scenes of smoking.* The thing that disturbs her about her dreams is not who turns up in them – her mother, a tutor she had at university, Beyle, the Dalai Lama, a child she saw today in the market – but how autonomous these people are. They appear to know their own minds. They act with an intelligence or anger or disinterest that cannot be hers but equally cannot be theirs, because they are not really them, so whose?

She passes small rooms without doors on both sides of a corridor. Men are sleeping on thin mattresses or just lying, watching her pass, waiting. Where are the women? There must be more than just the woman in the sari who was filling the water barrel, so where are they hiding? Behind the cardboard boxes? *Inside* the cardboard boxes?

John is both there and not there, ahead of her, in the shadows, flickering, and she's slow, because of her shoes. There is a smell of cooking and marijuana. In the last room along the corridor, on the side opposite the open yard, Beyle is lying on a mattress. Beneath a grey blanket he is wearing an army overcoat and his face is lathered in sweat. The pillow is wet. His face is towards her, his blue eyes open, but he doesn't recognise her. There are flies circling. She goes to the window and pushes it, pushes it again, hard, until something gives and the window opens. She looks out over fields of stubble to the runway of the airport, where a plane is taking off. She thinks of the passengers belted into their upright seats, and the little packets of food wrapped in foil delivered to their fold-down trays, and when she wakes her own pillow is wet too, though she has no memory of having wept.°

° 'I dreamt I was reading Stendhal in the Civitavecchia Nuclear Station: a shadow was sliding across the tiles of the reactors. It's Stendhal's ghost, said a young man in boots, naked from the waist up. And who are you? I asked. I'm the tile junkie, the hussar of tiles and shit, he said.' – Roberto Bolaño, *Tres*.

■ On her second day of following Henri B in Venice, Sophie Calle, wearing her blonde wig, is herself followed by an unknown man. On her fourth day she discovers where Henri B is staying. On her seventh day she finally sees him. For an hour she follows Henri B and his female companion through a maze of streets and alleys, taking photographs of them along the way, including one of B himself taking a photograph. In the evening she follows him again, until he and the woman go into an antiques shop and don't come out. After two hours of waiting outside in the cold (it's February), Calle asks a passing stranger to enter the shop and report back on what is happening; her reason, she explains, is that she is in love with the man ('only love seems admissable'). On the eighth day she follows Henri B again, another meander through the winding streets until, becoming aware of her presence, he turns and recognises her: 'Your eyes, I recognise your eyes; that's what you should have hidden.' They walk and take a vaporetto together, making desultory conversation. ('What did I imagine? That he was going to take me with him, to challenge me, to use me? Henri B did nothing. I discovered nothing.') They separate. Calle goes to the carnival, dances, spends the night on a bench with a harlequin. On the ninth and tenth days she watches Henri B's hotel entrance from the window of an upper room in a nearby house. She learns the reasons for Henri B's trip to Venice: to scout locations for a film and to take photographs 'for a book by C, the English writer'. On the eleventh day she learns that B and his partner will be returning to Paris by train that night. She finds another train, via Bologna, that will arrive in Paris five minutes before B's train. The following morning, in Paris, she photographs Henri B 'one last time as he passes through the station gate'.°

° For another of her projects, Calle photocopied the contents of an address book she found in the street before returning it to its owner, and then followed this stranger by contacting the people named in the address book and asking them to tell her about him: 'I will try to discover who he is without ever meeting him.' He is described by the people Calle meets as loyal, unselfish, perhaps lonely. 'He loves minor literature, B-movies, serialised 19th-century novels . . .' 'Without writing a novel about it, he is someone who is perfectly capable of disappearing without a trace.' 'When he leaves a message on your answerphone, it's always very confused. He's not good at condensing ideas.' 'He wasn't exactly the person he would have liked to be.' 'He's systematically ready to fall in love, on the condition that he doesn't stand a chance.' 'He wears clothes which are a little bit out of shape – always this black double-breasted alpaca coat.'

3

■ Starting cloudy, sunshine later, occasional showers.

Buying plums and a plum-coloured scarf in the market, Beyle suspects that he's being charged tourists' prices, but there's little point in arguing. Even though he'll be here for ever,° there'll always be people who'll regard him as an outsider.

Seeing a woman texting in a car stopped at traffic lights, Beyle asks himself why she is sitting in the back. The car is black and larger than it has need to be. The woman is blonde, in her thirties, looks a little glum so might be rich. She runs a bank or two, or a team of contract killers. The man driving the car is younger and wearing smart casual – jacket, open-necked blue shirt. No cap but still, no question, a chauffeur – discreet, eyes to the front – and the woman, Beyle thinks, re-imagining others' lives as if they weren't already imagined enough, is the man's boss. She asks him to do things, and he does them. Makes coffee, books tickets, looks things up. Sends flowers? Keeps secrets; is paid well,

---

° For ever is a long time. For ever is *deep* time, beyond time, not time at all, it's a gust of wind on a quiet day or nothing really, an intolerably high-density nothing. No end. No full stop. No right of reply.

or enough. She owns him: there is nothing he will not do. To an extent, he also owns her, because of those secrets. A glance from her into the rear-view mirror and he will expertly slide into the back of this elongated car and no less expertly kneel and raise her dress and peel down her tights and begin licking her.

Later in the day, while riding a bus, Beyle has a sudden feeling of *omniscience*. Or, more crudely, *power* – he could stand on a beach and tell the tide to turn back and it would. He could hijack this bus right now and no one could stop him, and he could tell the driver to drive to any place he wanted, somewhere beyond the mere exercise of power.

Then a cloud scuds across the sun and he feels as if he has run a marathon or dug six graves in frozen ground – his body has done its bit and now the mind is free to sing its own song but the mind too would prefer to just curl up.

The woman sitting behind him keeps sneezing. The woman sitting beside him is eating noodles out of a styro-foam tray. Beyle has eaten nothing all day except half a croissant.

The matter of love. The matter of France. The matter of the plumber and his mate and the leaking toilet. Something about trees . . .

■ Astronauts – no: divers, frogmen – are bobbing about in the water, and police cars and ambulances with disco lights are parked along the riverside and yellow tape is fluttering around the whole scene. People are standing along the river bank and on the bridge, watching, shrugging. They seem unsure if what they are here for has already happened or is still to come. Among them a man is saying something, anything, and being believed for as far as he goes. A dog is splashing in the water among the divers.

A girl has fallen off a tourist boat into the water, or thrown herself off, and has probably drowned.

A plastic bottle floats by, stops, floats on, and Beyle stares at the place where it stopped, focusing hard until the water starts to turn, slowly at first but picking up speed, and a whirlpool forms, drilling down, at its centre a pillar of air, and at the bottom of the whirlpool, tangled among stones and weeds, is the body of a girl dressed in jeans and a yellow jacket, her brown hair like the skin of an otter.

This is a thing Beyle can do, though he hasn't chosen it. Anne-Lise Bouvier, 16; from Brussels; two older sisters, one brother; ambition, to become an eye surgeon. (Another thing Beyle can do – implausibly, but this gift *was* among those he expressly asked for, and it does help if you happen to be writing in English about a Frenchman – is speak and understand any language he desires.)°

° In April 1840 Beyle compiled a list of 'Privileges' he wished to be granted. These included: no more than three days of illness per year; hardness of his penis whenever he wanted (and thickness the same but length two inches more than at the time of writing); a ring which, when touched while he is looking at a woman, will cause

If you had a special talent, Beyle says – say, you could walk on water –

Or turn water into wine, adds Anna enthusiastically, lying beside Beyle in his single bed, most of her still wrapped around him to avoid falling out. Her sweat, his dryness: complementary.

---

the woman to fall in love with him (or, if the ring is slightly moistened with saliva, become just a devoted friend); another ring that will destroy all lice, fleas and other parasites within a radius of six metres, and cause wild animals to flee; fine hair, good skin, agreeable body odour; each morning, a gold coin in his pocket plus some loose change in the currency of whichever country he happens to be in; the licence to kill ten people a year; the ability to reduce the pain of someone he sees by three-quarters, and/or prolong their life by ten days; the ability to see what anyone he chooses (*but not the woman he loves*) is doing at that moment; the ability to make someone forget him; twice a day, simply by praying for food, the immediate appearance of bread, a well-done steak, a leg of lamb, a plate of spinach, a bottle of good wine and a carafe of water, plus fruit, ice cream and coffee; the ability to travel to wherever he wants at a speed of 100 leagues per hour (and during the journey, sleep); the ability to become someone else (and so occupy two bodies at the same time). Plus, a prohibition on revealing any of these privileges to any other person – if he tried to do so, his voice would be silenced and he would suffer toothache for twenty-four hours.

So as not to ask *too much* from whatever supernatural agent might be expected to grant these requests, Beyle tempers them with curbs or nods towards realism: brilliance at cards and billiards, for example, but winnings limited to no more than 100 francs. Most of the privileges were to be enjoyed on only so many occasions per year. He was not being unreasonable.

You might not want this to be widely known, Beyle continues, you might want to keep it to yourself. People would think you a freak, they would be afraid of you.

Romance would be hard, says Anna. And you'd have wait till night-time to do your walking on water, to avoid being seen. And then what would be the point?

■ In his twenties Poverino was a struggling artist, and at fifty-two he's still an artist but no longer a struggling one, because who at that age can wake up every morning with the prospect of nothing but *struggle*? But still, occasionally . . . Yesterday evening, while walking in the run-down area around the old slaughterhouse – the new one is further out, and fully automated – he had an idea for a painting, a painting so far in advance of anything he has done before it will change his life.

He hardly slept. But he can't start today, even though he's up early and his vision is still intact, because today he is meeting his sister to discuss whether they should hire a home-help for their mother or whether it's time to move her into a care home. His sister, whom he sees only twice a year at most, is married to a banker. His sister has never lacked for anything. She has chosen a restaurant in the centre of town, and walking towards it along a street lined with fashion shops – "le *Bondstreet*, la rue à la mode" – he is stirred by a memory: this was the shop, surely, in whose window all those years ago he once saw an overcoat, a most elegant coat, that he promised himself he would buy from the proceeds of his first gallery exhibition. The shop has changed hands, many times. He has never had a solo exhibition. Someone else is wearing his coat.

In the restaurant he mentions the coat to his sister. She too remembers that shop but no, it was in a different street. It's now a sushi bar.

She's wrong, he'd bet on it. They always have these arguments, the artist and his sister; they can never agree about anything.

■ From the window of his room at the Aramis, Beyle sees a child walking down the middle of the street dressed as a witch, with a canoe paddle as a broomstick.° It's spotting with rain. Posses of tourists wearing pacamaks and carrying colourful umbrellas remind him of boiled sweets wrapped in cellophane.

Behind Beyle, Anna is giggling in bed. He wants to tell her about the child dressed as a witch, and maybe about the person not yet born, but not while she is laughing.

Often he doesn't know whether she's listening to him

° Beyle in Toulouse, 28 March 1838: "As I came out I met a peasant woman carrying a peacock in a basket on her head. His splendid tail hung down fully three feet over the basket . . . A hundred feet further on I came upon a little ten-year-old priest in collar, tricorn hat and cassock. His mother was leading him by the hand."

or not. Sometimes he rubs his fingers just below his chin, where his beard would be if he had a beard. Sometimes he closes his eyes and feels his insides squirming like worms in a bucket of bait. Was it any easier in the old days?°

Is it only if you're a writer, he says – and a writer is what he'd like to be, with some degree of celebrity, just the right amount – as if that was his to choose – that when you're in love you're interested less in the moonshine than the awkwardness and humiliations involved? What do you think?

Sorry? says Anna, taking off her headphones.

Unless she is sharing her bed, Anna can't go to sleep without some noise in the background. She assumes that what's apparent is all there is to know, but she is still curious. How many words in a novel? 66,000, Beyle says, and she frowns as if she's been short-changed. Why in French are love and death the same word? No, for *l'amour* you pout your lips, like this. Why does Beyle have so many names for himself? If he is trying to protect his real name – like the name of God, too precious to be spoken aloud – then protect it from what or from who?

Beyle's relationship with M is to Anna a puzzle. If he really does love her, surely he wants for her what she wants

---

° In September 1835, in the dust on a path on the shore of a lake south of Rome, Beyle scrawled the intitials of twelve women he had loved and pondered "on the astonishing follies and stupidities they made me do (I say astonishing for me, not for the reader, and anyway I don't repent of them)".

for herself, even if that is not him – why can't he be happy with that? Beyle says that's what he does want for her, and he's told her.° There's more to this than he's letting on, but the expression on his face tells Anna that he'd prefer not to talk more, not now.

Nor does Anna understand how this man was once put in charge of organising supplies for a whole army, it just doesn't seem a job he's cut out for. If he knows so many important people, why can't he be paid just to be happy?

Ah, says Beyle, that word again.

In the street the witch-child is having a spitting competition with two other children.

'Shall we go for a walk?' Anna suggests. The rain is now coming down hard.°°

■ Guitar lessons, driving lessons, yoga, rooms for rent, men with vans, laptop repairs, escorts for any occasion: from a selection of these a whole life could be stitched together. Beyle turns from the noticeboard and sees M's sister sitting alone at a table. He introduces himself.

You have your idea of a person, or even yourself, and then

° Beyle to Mathilde in August 1819: "Farewell, madame, be happy. I do not believe that you can be, except if you love. Be happy, even if loving another than myself." Fine words, says Anna.

°° *Armance*: "It was raining in torrents; the rain delighted him."

they've been hacked into by someone else. Yes, she broke up with a lover, but people do. No one drowned, no one was burned alive. About Japanese food she is neutral: usually no, but sometimes nothing else will do. As for whatever M might have told Beyle about her, M is fond of telling stories – ask her what she had for breakfast and she'll tell you about the new food scares or super-fruits, she'll never just say *toast*. No mention is made of the dog.

'There are women,' M's sister says, 'and there are women', and Beyle is thinking about this – it comes across as a kind of warning; quotation marks are implied around one of those two sets of women, but if not women, what are they? – when he notices a tiny camera fixed to the ceiling of the café, a camera that is pointed towards the table they are sitting at.° He winks at the the camera, fishes an envelope from his pocket, and starts to write on its back – a message in code? The symbol for infinity? One of his little maps with As and Bs and wobbly lines? He'll be disappointed if there's no film in the camera.

° The all-seeeing eye was supposed to be that of God. If the temporal authorities wished to take over the job, Beyle was happy to play cat-and-mouse with them. His aliases, his digressions and interruptions, his notes scribbled in code: his whole way of life was *calculated* to attract suspicion. He lived in hotels and rented rooms; he was always booking a seat in a stagecoach setting off for somewhere else (and starting a new job, a new book, a new love affair). The plots of his novels thrive on conspiracies, disguises, secret

■ Beyle quotes an acquaintance whose daughter died at the age of thirteen: "To me it's as if my daughter were in America."°

■ In the airport departures hall M hears her name announced over the public address system and this request: would she please come to the information desk, where her mother is waiting. Her mother is dead, but the message reminds her to buy sweets for her children to suck when the plane takes off. She remembers the flickering noise that used to be made by the departures board after a plane took off and all the cities shuffled upwards.

And at the other end, exiting into the arrivals hall, the

---

messages. He prefaced his memoir *The Life of Henry Brulard* with a note "To Messrs of the Police" assuring them that the book was a novel, written in imitation of Goldsmith's *The Vicar of Wakefield* and narrated by a hero who was once married to Charlotte Corday, assassin of Marat (and therefore politically conservative, no one to scratch their heads over). In a police report dated May 1815 Beyle is described as "a stout lad, born at Grenoble, aged 31, lodging at Rue Neuve du Luxembourg no. 3 . . . He goes frequently to the theatre and always lives with some actress or other . . . He buys many books and comes home at midnight" – a report written by himself, to save the police the trouble.

° Beyle himself had no wish to go to America. "Americans are merely the quintessence of the English, harder workers, greedier, more pious, on the whole more unpleasant."

often handwritten and mis-spelled names° held up in the arrivals hall by drivers of a certain age who are heavy smokers, many of them, and who by rights should have died or at least retired to the Costa Wherever but who instead are used to this waiting, this waiting, this waiting, for flights that *for technical reasons* have been delayed.

■ Midnight. Out of the goodness of his heart, a bruised and troubled organ, Beyle is waiting up at the reception desk for a guest whose train has been delayed. The TV on the wall, turned to mute, is showing a game show. A lone fish sulks in the tabletop aquarium. Beyle is poking the tuning button on a radio, hoping to find some late Cimarosa, when he hears seagulls – not from the radio, not ready-made gulls from the sound-effects library spliced in after the lovers lie down in the dunes, but actual gulls.

It's true the town is nowhere near the sea but on windy days gulls are blown inland. Or they come for the weekend: gulls can tire of just *sea*. They gather in the park near the

---

° The names Beyle and Franco write down in the ledger on the desk in the Hotel Aramis, checking in, checking out. The names of the three gloomy fish in the tabletop aquarium: Harpo, Chico and the other one. Lupetto, the name of one of the two dogs to which Beyle was devoted in the last year of his life ("I was being saddened by having nothing to love"), a lively dog; the other, a black English spaniel, "sad and melancholic", name not known.

bandstand, quarrelling over the litter bins. They blitz the picnicking tourists.

Beyle stands in the open doorway of the Aramis. A tourist, a little drunk, asks him directions to one of the twenty-three churches and Beyle says the church is closed. All of them? the man asks. All of them. A child who should be in bed at this hour offers him a peppermint and Beyle declines, he doesn't accept sweets from strange children, and then changes his mind and the child asks him what he's doing here. He's in love, Beyle says, knowing not to lie to children. And because (a) the woman he's in love with doesn't love him back, and (b) love is not a tap you can simply turn on or off, then (c) he seems to be stuck.

Oh, says the child – boy? girl? It's difficult to tell – he'll get over it.

Beyle so hates that expression that he spits out the peppermint into the gutter.

The telephone rings at the reception desk and Beyle goes back inside to pick up. It's the woman on the train to say don't bother about waiting up, it turns out she's on the wrong train anyway.

He leafs through a tile catalogue that the plumber has delivered: the plain ones, the ones with decorative elements (leaves, fish, arabesques), the beige, the maroon, the green. He is leaning towards the pale green.

On the table by the tourist brochures, someone has left a pair of sunglasses.

■ She led an exemplary life. Or perhaps she poisoned her own children, Horace Smith doesn't know, but the former is statistically more likely. The only things Smith does know about Mary Roberts are that she was born in 1948 and died in 2003 and she 'enjoyed this view'.

Not much of a view: a patch of grass, two or three trees, a litter bin, another bin in which dog-walkers drop their dogs' mess in little plastic bags, and beyond those more bins, recycling ones, and then a Waitrose, a café with outdoor seating, a row of charity shops.

The bench inscribed for Mary Roberts was intended for another location, Smith came to believe, but that view was popular, a best-selling view, and all the benches were taken, so her family had to make do with here. Smith grew fond of that bench. There was a period – a summer so dry that he cannot remember any rain – when he worked abroad but sometimes had to come back to London, and he was in love with a woman who wasn't so in love with him, but she must have been at least a bit, because whenever he arrived in London and called her she would come to the hotel where he was staying. Or, if she hadn't the time to come to his hotel, if her husband was at home or she had to help her children with their homework or make supper for guests and she was running late, they would meet at this *green*, as she called it, which was close to where she lived. They would meet at this bench.

It was only after little gaps were opening up in what they had to say to each other that Smith accepted it wasn't their bench at all, it was Mary Roberts's bench, her name carved into the back-rest, though the woman had known this earlier. She was letting him down gently, as was her manner. She was letting him know that without a bed, they had only this bench, and its view was not good. She had her house and her husband and her recipe books and her children and their homework, and he had a rented flat in Brussels and a pocketful of loose change in which the pounds and pence were always mixed up with euros, so that the shopkeepers of London would look at what he'd offered and shake their heads. As did the woman, in the end.

A couple of years later, Smith was introduced at a party to a woman named Mary Roberts. She wasn't a bit like he'd imagined her. She was a financial analyst with KPMG. 'I've heard so much about you,' she said to Smith. You shouldn't be able, he told her, to dedicate a bench in a beauty spot to a loved one in perpetuity, there are only so many beauty spots, only so many benches, not enough to hold everyone in fond memory. There should be a time limit.

■ In just a few months, Napoleon will be found dead of hypothermia behind the bus station. Of his dog, not a hair nor a flea. John will drift north and west; he'll be locked up and released, locked up and released; his grandchildren will be doctors and engineers. Anna, devoutly religious, will have nine children by three different partners and will be loved by all. Franco will spend ten years writing a revisionist history of the twentieth century based on the premise that Gavrilo Princip, supposed assassin of Archduke Franz Ferdinand of Austria in Sarajevo in June 1914, *missed*. M will be knocked down by joyriders in a stolen car; her daughter will fly to her hospital bedside and will be appalled by M's saying, just before she dies, that she has *served her purpose*. It's as if her mother is taking revenge. M's son will move to California and work in surveillance; he will become a billionaire by developing Afterlife, an online virtual world whose users' avatars are defined by the continuously updated data recorded of their actual lives.°

■ I lose sight of him for a while but then there he is, off on a long jog that takes him out of the town and into a forest. He is fitter now than he was only a few weeks ago. His fluorescent shoes are well muddied. There are painted signs on the trees – trail markers, blazes – to guide him

---

° *Based on a true story.* Mathilde Dembowski died in 1825. Beyle noted the date of her death in a copy of *De l'Amour* and added, in English, "Death of the author". If the author was himself, this was premature: his novels were still to come. Or *she* was the author, of Beyle's hope and despair. Beyle's sister Pauline died in 1857 in poverty, her husband having died many years before. She worked as an attendant at the spa baths of Enghien-les-Bains. She inherited a small amount of money from the sale of Beyle's books and clothes – which included sixteen shirts, four waistcoats, a pair of braces and an overcoat.

and bring him safely back home: another dotted line. The markers, according to the leaflet from the tourist information office, are not widely spaced, so if he doesn't see one for some time he'll know that he's gone off track, which is helpful in a way that offers no help at all. What does 'not widely spaced' actually mean? How will he know whether he is lost or not lost?°

A deer scoots across the path. Overhead, a plane is flying south ('held aloft by the internal force of its style, as the earth stays aloft on its own'). M will be at home now, doing whatever she does: walking from room to room, dressing to go out to the opera, reading the *LRB*, writing an email, conspiring to free Milan from the yoke of Austrian oppression.

He has a favourite tree.°° If he were to lie down beside this tree and fall asleep, a wolf would step out of the forest and sniff him.

In a clearing – a perfect spot for a duel°°° – he comes across a wooden seat raised high on stilts and nailed to

---

° In 1822, unable to sit alone in his room, Beyle took the proofs of *De l'Amour* ("printed in duodecimo on poor paper") into the countryside at Montmorency. "In the middle of the woods, especially on the left of the sandpit as you climb up, I used to correct my proofs. I nearly went mad."

°° As did Fabrizio in *La Chartreuse de Parme*, a chestnut.

°°° Beyle's advice on duels, as recorded by Prosper Mérimée: "When you are being aimed at, look at a tree, and apply yourself to the task of counting the leaves."

a tree trunk, with a rickety ladder up to the seat, and he climbs this ladder and surveys the view and ponders a life as a forestry worker: a cottage with a wood-burning stove and Anna in the kitchen cooking dumplings while listening to Scandinavian bands on her iPhone. Or a life back in Paris, his Anna an actress who dies every night on stage before coming home and to bed at number 3, rue Neuve du Luxembourg.

Deep in the forest there are tiny domed chapels. The windows are barred and the doors locked with rusty padlocks, but each time Beyle stumbles across one of these chapels it shows signs of recent entry: lit candles, the floor newly swept, a prayer still lingering in the air, fading.

Beyle often feels as if he has got away with something, escaped scot free, though from what he'd find it hard to say. He is also a little afraid, but this is what forests are for.

■ In windy weather, one may lose one's hat.° *I went home to get my hat. A complete stranger asked me for a cigarette. Whatever you say, I will make its price all right for you.* However sad it may seem, it is quite certain he is mad. *Driver, I want to go to sleep for a little; when we have arrived somewhere, please wake me.* It would be something to know where we are going to. *Wherever you go, you will see strange things.* Most

---

° Alternating sentences: see note on page 39.

dogs are faithful animals. *Come inside; I have some unusual things to show you.* She was seen coming out of the house by two men who were passing by. *Boy, where have you put my pen and blotting paper?* No one can ever foresee what he will do next. *I am feeling very ill; please give me a little medicine.* It is doubtful if he means to marry. *Sir, however much we have searched, we have not found the spades.* Afterwards, when he had gone, his overcoat was found.

III Eternal City

In 1828 Beyle was aged forty-five, unemployed, cast aside by the woman he loved (another one: Countess Clémentine Curial, the one who in 1824 kept him locked in the cellar of her chateau for three days and herself climbed down a ladder with food and water and up again with his chamber-pot), and thinking (again) about suicide. He needed money, work, distraction. His cousin arrived in Paris with notes for a travel book on Rome, and travel guides made money (in *La Chartreuse de Parme* he's alert to an English book on Italy, translated into French in 1826, "which has gone into a twentieth edition because it lists for the prudent English-man the price of a guinea-fowl, an apple, a glass of milk").

A year later Beyle published *Promenades dans Rome* (*A Roman Journal*), a book of many hundred pages:

> From the table on which I am writing I can see three-fourths of Rome; and across from me, at the other end of town, the cupola of St Peter's rises majestically. In the evening, I per-ceive the setting sun through the windows of St Peter's, and a half-hour later this admirable dome is outlined against the exquisitely pure glow of an orange-hued twilight surmounted high up in the sky by some star that is just appearing.

Etcetera. The actual table at which the book on Rome was written was in a room at the Hôtel de Valois, 71 rue de Richelieu, Paris. Beyle is, among other things, the patron saint of hack writers. And just as, as he noted, "St Lawrence never walks about without having at his side a small grille which recalls the one on which he suffered martyrdom; St Catherine always carries a wheel; St Sebastian bears arrows, etc.", let Beyle have beside him a heap of reference books, black coffee, speed, a candle burning at both ends. He doesn't need a halo. The halo, he guessed, is simply "the imitation of an electric effect that some young novice may have observed before daylight, on awakening for matins a venerable old man lying in woollen sheets".

In the same way that he peppered his autobiographical writings with diagrams and maps, a show of authenticity, Beyle includes in the Rome book facts and figures in finer detail than anyone could ever need. The Colosseum: "its total height is 157 feet, and its outer circumference is 1,641 feet. The arena in which the gladiators fought is 285 feet in length by 182 in width." There are lists, including one of his favourite twenty-two churches. There are detailed descriptions of architecture, paintings, sculptures, and discussions of the emperors and the popes. The genre requires this. There are also extended riffs on music, love, poisoning, banditry, holy relics (including the foreskin of Jesus) and the national characteristics of the Italians, the Germans, the Spanish and the French. There is advice on giving bribes ("The moment you see a police or customs officer, you take a twenty-*soldi* coin and play with it in such a way that he can see it") and how generally to make your visit hassle-free: "You can avoid trouble everywhere by claiming illness, by going to mass every day and never losing your temper."

And more: Beyle is travelling, supposedly, with companions – four men, three women – and the book is written in the form of a journal that recounts their sightseeing and also their visits to concerts and theatres and soirées and their picnics and the stories they are told. One of the men, Frederick, "the German character", forty-six years old, has "a firm and profound mind that nothing dazzles"; another is Paul, aged thirty, "who loves sallies, the clash of views, the rapid rattle of conversation". Paul "cannot bear" the Colosseum: "He claims that these ruins bore him or make him ill." The two other men are "of a rather serious turn of mind". Of the women, one likes Mozart and Beyle is hopeful: "I am quite sure that she will like Coreggio."

This is halfway (less than halfway, in truth, but moving in this direction) towards being a novel. In 1827, the year before he wrote the Rome book, Beyle had published his first novel proper – though, backing off, he claimed in the preface that *Armance* was written by "a woman of character, who has only a vague idea of what constitutes literary merit", and he himself was present only to "correct the style", and his habitual fondness for disguise resulted in his main character's distinguishing feature (impotence) being so coded that readers were baffled.

Tethered to Rome, *Promenades dans Rome* is free improvisation; 'the book seems to be written,' Giuseppe di Lampedusa noted, 'entirely by itself.' The entry for 4 December 1828 includes an anecdote about the disastrous first night of Rossini's *The Barber of Seville* in Rome in 1816; the entry for 12 December is given over to observations on the "facial tranquillity" of Roman women ("A Roman woman looks at the face of the man who is speaking to her as, in the morning, in the country, you look at a mountain"). Between them, on 10 December, there is a commotion in the street. A man – a miller's apprentice – is running: he has just killed his wife's lover, a rich merchant. Beyle and his party follow him, and when he collapses on the steps of a church they rent a room with a window overlooking the scene. Suddenly, between the killer and the police, who are waiting for permission to make an arrest on the church steps, a crowd of onlookers bursts in, and the killer vanishes.

If Beyle didn't feel it necessary to travel to Rome in order to write a book about it, he wasn't relying entirely on the knowledge of others. He'd been there, and would go again, most frequently during the last decade of his life, 1831–42, when he held the position of consul in the port town of Civitavecchia, "this little hole of seven thousand five hundred inhabitants". Rome was only fifty miles away. Rome had art, music, disputation, pretty women, street-life. He kept lodgings there throughout this period.

In Rome in the summer of 1832 Beyle considers writing a memoir of his life during the previous decade. The idea is both appealing ("What kind of man am I? . . . Am I good or bad, clever or stupid?") and appalling ("the number of my shirts, the misfortunes of my ego"). But vanity is not the main worry; he isn't writing for publication, not in his lifetime, and besides, "such books are like all others: quickly forgotten if boring". The issue, as always with Beyle, is happiness: his fear of "deflowering" the moments and periods of happiness that he'd experienced by writing about them. Solution: "I'll skip them." He writes flat-out for two weeks (*Souvenirs d'Egotisme*) and then stops: there's a heatwave, and "it's become too hot to think".

In 1835, before embarking on another memoir (*La Vie de Henry Brulard*), Beyle scribbles with a stick on a path by the lake at Albano the names of the women he has loved. A wind will wipe them. Not their real names; just the initials of the names he has given them. Beyle's habit of assigning false names not just to himself but to those he loved was a way of insulating happiness from chat, gossip, writing; perhaps also, a way of keeping these women semi-fictional, at arm's length.

Although he has certain official duties – which include keeping a record of ships entering and leaving the harbour – much of Beyle's time during this last decade is spent pottering about (a rehearsal for the afterlife). He goes on an archaeological dig and sends some fragments of Etruscan vases to a woman friend in Paris: "The pottery is of a handsome black, and can be used for serving your tea." He complains of the tedium and "vast maliciousness" of small towns; in Civitavecchia, "The women spend their time dreaming of ways to make their husbands give them a hat from France." He contemplates death by boredom. He proposes marriage to a twenty-year-old girl; when he realises that the girl's father intends to move in with them, he backs off. He pays for copies to be made of some late Renaissance manuscripts he finds in an archive – daggers, blood, incest, vengeance – and embarks on his own versions of these. He starts other projects – novels, memoirs – and moves from one to the next without finishing any of them.

"I have gout and gravel, I am very fat, excessively nervous and fifty years of age." He is, basically, past it, whatever *it* was (*"Qu'est-que ça?"*). But not entirely so. On leave in Paris at the start of November 1838, he instructs the concierge to tell anyone who calls that he's away hunting and begins dictating a new book; he finishes it on 26 December, and *La Chartreuse de Parme* is published the following March. In fifty-three days he has forged the contradictions of a lifetime – lyricism and worldliness, sunlight and shadow – into a new kind of novel. Does he know that he has written a masterpiece? ("I regard, and have always regarded, my works as lottery tickets.") How could he not? But when, back in Civitavecchia, he receives a copy of the *Revue Parisienne* with Balzac's admiring sixty-page review, he is dumbfounded: "Your amazing article, such as no writer has ever received from another, caused me – I now confess it – to burst into laughter as I read it, whenever I came upon a somewhat excessive piece of praise, which I did at every step."

Steeped in history, Rome is steeped in blood. In *A Time in Rome* Elizabeth Bowen notes that of the the twelve rulers who followed Augustus, founder of the Roman Empire, 'seven died by violence. Their existences were nervous and ostentatious. They encaged the Palatine in marble, over which ran blood, more than once their own.' For Bowen as novelist, the city was simply too big, too *there*, too concentrated a gathering of history and at the same time proliferating, unmanageable: 'The idea of putting Rome into a novel not only did not attract me, it shocked me – *background*, for heaven's sake! The thing was a major character, out of scale with any fictitious cast.'

By which she meant, I think, life in the midst of death, death in the midst (or mist) of life, and Rome hammers this home and you can't disentangle them and for the kind of novels she wrote, so finely poised, so delighting in social comedy, Rome would have been too obtrusive. Emmeline, when she first meets Markie in Bowen's *To the North*, is in a train travelling north from Milan, an altogether milder place (though not to Beyle), and Rome is reduced to gossip: 'Mark's Rome was late Renaissance, with a touch of the slick modernity of *Vogue*.'

Writers do set novels in Rome, of course. Bowen was overawed. Rilke was not: writing from Rome in 1903, he complained of 'the unspeakable excess of esteem, nourished by academics and philologists with the help of run-of-the-mill tourists, given to all these disfigured and spoilt objects which after all are basically nothing more than accidental vestiges of another age and of a life that is not our own and is not meant to be'. Rome has no more claim to eternity than Thebes or Tenochtitlan or the Uxbridge Road. "The streets of Rome," Beyle noted in 1826, "are infected with an odour of rotten cabbage."

Leaving aside Henry James, the first of three Roman novels that come immediately to mind – and the number three feels right: it's embedded deep in folklore, magic, religion, jokes – is Alfred Hayes' *The Girl on the Via Flaminia* (1949). After the liberation of Rome in 1944 – for its citizens a period of massive deprivation, when 'a suit bankrupted a family, a shirt starved the children, an overcoat cost more than a funeral' – an American soldier takes a room in a house that comes with a girl: he gets sex and release from the awfulness of barracks life, she gets a roof over her head and as much chocolate and as many cigarettes as she wants. An embittered English soldier denounces this house to the public authorities. The girl has to get registered officially as a sex worker, bureaucratically humiliated. She runs. The American, loving her, runs after her: 'He ran toward the city.'

In Wolfgang Koeppen's *Death in Rome*, written in the early 1950s, there is both death and – like something that happens off-stage which we learn about only years later, which in fact cannot be known until another death makes it knowable – a stopping. The death on the last page of the book is that of a monstrous former Nazi general, survivor of 'a war that was far from over, or that hadn't properly begun yet'. He is contemptuous of Rome: 'The eternal city, they called it. That was professors' and priests' talk. Judejahn showed his murderer's face. He knew better than that. He'd seen plenty of cities go under.' The stopping is that of the author: though he lived for another forty years and discussed a range of subjects and accepted advances from his publisher and repeatedly agreed on deadlines, he never wrote another novel.

Carlo Emilio Gadda's *That Awful Mess on the Via Merulana* (1957) is a rambunctious shaggy dog story, the meandering investigation of two crimes (a robbery, a murder) in a single block of flats by a grumpy police officer who is hampered not least by his own philosophising – his belief that behind every cause or motive is another, an infinite series, and his attribution of 'a soul, indeed a lousy bastard of a soul, to that system of forces and probabilities which surrounds every human creature, and is customarily called destiny'. Gossip, rumours, lies and false leads accumulate. No surprise that the book ends without any solution to the crimes, or to 'the wicked mystery of this world'.

Fulsome in his praise for *La Chartreuse*, Balzac reserved his right to nitpick. For a new edition, the early part could do with cutting; more physical description of the characters, please; the ending needed more development. Beyle took him seriously ("the King of Novelists of this century"). He received a copy of Balzac's review late on 15 October 1840; in the first of three drafts of a letter thanking Balzac, dated the following day, he claimed that he had already reduced the first fifty-four pages to just four or five.

But Beyle's draft letters are also defensive. "Often I ponder for a quarter of an hour whether to place an adjective before or after its noun. I seek to be (1) truthful, (2) clear in my accounts of what happens in a human heart . . ." Once upon a time he used to plan his novels, but now "drawing up plans freezes me stiff". The tensions between surprise and gratitude and stubbornness are evident in every impatient press of the paragraph key. Mercifully, the impulse to reconfigure *La Chartreuse* acccording to another writer's notions of how a novel should be written soon lapsed.

Truthfulness and clarity: slippery things, and not always compatible. Obvious strategies are avoidance of clichés and fine writing: "As for beauty of phraseology, its roundness, rhythm, etc., I often regard it as a fault . . . Whilst writing the *Chartreuse*, in order to acquire the correct tone I occasionally read a few pages of the *Code civil* . . . Style cannot be too *clear*, too *simple*." (This last was his beef with Balzac, which he expressed more openly elsewhere: he suggested that Balzac wrote his novels twice, "the first time rationally, and the second time he dresses them up in this beautiful neological style, full of the sufferings of the soul".) What counts more, perhaps, is how for Beyle the habit of story-telling is second nature, *first* nature even, partaking of his lifelong conviction that from childhood to death the constant negotiation between self and society (or between the cool restraints of Classicism and whatever is being restrained, which includes the Romantic imperatives) involves artfulness and deception: lies, codes, fantasy, secrecy, feints, bluff, dissimulation – the basic stuff of fiction. Most people, Giuseppi Lampedusa suggests, read the *Chartreuse* as a thriller.

About the ending, Balzac was bound to suggest what he did. The story, if story is the thing, essentially ends (in English, in the Penguin Classics edition) two-thirds of the way down page 502, almost off-stage, with "a well-known voice saying, very quietly, 'Come in, friend of my heart.'" *Entre ici, ami de mon cœur.* The voice is that of Clelia, in darkness, who has made a vow never to set eyes on Fabrizio again. Next page, permission is asked of the reader to pass over "a gap of three years". Within the following five pages – a wrap-up – their child dies, Clelia dies, Fabrizio makes a will (sums of money spelt out, typically Beyle) and enters the Charterhouse of Parma (a monastery, never previously mentioned) and dies, the Countess Sanseverina dies, the state prospers. *Le Rouge and le Noir* concludes with a similar dash towards the finishing line: within the two final pages Julien is executed, Mathilde de la Mole kisses his severed head and buries it, marble carvings are ordered from Italy at huge expense, and Madame de Rênal dies.

Exhaustion, elation. Let the thing be finished, but with the least possible authorial agency. Let it go.

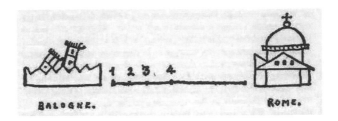

BOLOGNE.   ROME.

Bologna (above) is indifference, Rome is perfect love. Supposedly, this diagram plots the progress of love (male perspective): 1 is admiration; 2 is oh, she's looking back, she's paying me attention; 3 is hope; 4 is "when one delights in overrating the beauty and merit of the woman one loves". It's an illustration of the theory of crystallisation that Beyle proposed in *De l'Amour*: the working of the mind in collaboration with physical attraction, the perception by the lover of irresistible qualities in the loved one that to an objective observer are invisible. The metaphor is taken from salt mines near Salzburg: a branch thrown into the mine is saturated with salt water which, drying, leaves the branch "with a shining deposit of crystals". Beyle was visiting the mines with a woman friend, La Ghita, who was given a crystallised branch by their guide; he watched a Bavarian cavalry officer becoming infatuated with her, to the point where he began praising her hand, which was in fact pockmarked from an episode of smallpox in childhood. The woman invited the Bavarian officer to lunch the following day; "whatever stupidity I happen to utter, I shall not cease to be perfect in the eyes of my handsome German: that's most convenient."

Later, discussing love with La Ghita in Bologna, Beyle drew the Bologna/Rome picture on the back of a playing card. What's immediately apparent is that even when stage four is reached, you're not even halfway to Rome.

Not all roads lead to Rome, but some do. (Harry Mathews: 'All Rome leads to roads.') I – writing this in June – plan to go there in September, and I was thinking, after I'd thought of ending this book with something Roman, that I'd write this bit *in* Rome, but it turns out I'm not patient enough to wait until September. I'm clearly intrigued more by the idea of Rome than the city itself; or by the idea of tourism as a form of the afterlife.°

Not much sightseeing, I think. Encounters with people who want to sell me things or tell me things. Little problems with exchange rates and bus tickets. If there's a funicular (and surely, with seven hills?), I'll take a ride on that. I will find – in a shoe box: I've dreamt this – a cache of Stend-halia: sketches, notes, letters, written in a code I will never decipher. I'll watch Monica Vitti trying on a new hat, even though she already has so many. I'll savour the grind and grumble of trams, I'll sit at outdoor tables at cafés near the

---

° In *Roma* by Marguerite Duras, a woman on a hotel terrace says, 'I'm afraid that Rome existed . . .' Her companion, male, echoes her: Rome existed. 'Are you sure . . .' Yes, he says; and the rivers, and all the rest. 'How can you stand that . . .'

river reading the minor works of long-dead major writers and it will feel, it already does, as if I'm in a small town not a big one. A pretty waitress, a gust of starlings rising above the pine trees at sunset, if you want to get *sepia* about this. It will rain and I'll get soaked. Not really knowing where I am, I will walk around in my sensible shoes.

Beyle would be scornful. He travelled constantly but recoiled from mass tourism, and wasn't surprised when his *Mémoires d'un Touriste* was not received kindly: it's hard, he remarked, to please fools with a book that spends 700 pages proving that that's what they are.

For the *Mémoires*, written for a flat but necessary fee in the year before the *Chartreuse*, Beyle adopted the persona of a widowed iron merchant who wants to explore the by-ways of France before he retires to Martinique. It's as if the Austrian Tourist Board had commissioned a book extolling their country by Thomas Bernhard.

From the very first entry (10 April 1837), Beyle is on edge: his servant is too talkative, and he swears that if ever he undertakes another journey like this one he'll choose a servant who doesn't speak French. Next paragraph: "I am getting over some frightfully ugly country. Long grey dull paths run to the horizon." Impatient with the uniformity of what passes for *opinion* in Paris, he's no less dismayed by the dreariness of the provinces: "The provincial still does not know that everything in life is a comedy." Much of the countryside is simply "depressing", many of the towns not much better: "all the time I am in this town I want to yawn".

Little praise that doesn't damn: in Geneva he visits the house where Rousseau was born, which has recently been rebuilt: "It is now a fine six-storey house like those which daily help to uglify Paris." Or: the chateau of Fontainebleau is "like a dictionary of architecture. Everything is there, but nothing is impressive." Or: "The houses of all the villages had just been whitewashed, which gave them an extraordinary air of cleanliness and gaiety, an air precisely of what they are not." As he travels south – and nearer to his beloved Italy – he cheers up, but this only makes him uneasy. A chateau on a hill is lovely, "but how can these things be described? I would have to take a high-flown epic tone for ten pages, and I have a horror of that." Walking in the cork forests near Perpignan, he finds that "everything pleased me" – and immediately adds: "Is it unwise to be this way?"

Meandering from one town to the next, Beyle documents "the incredible and hereditary asinity of the mayors and magistrates of France". He advises an innkeeper on how to get milk from an egg, and the burghers of Nantes on how to grow better trees. He recounts stories: the tale of the Englishman, Mr Smith, whose suicide attempt failed because he'd bought his prussic acid not from his regular pharmacist, who he suspected was overcharging him, but from a cheaper one; the tale of the German traveller who, noticing that his friend was keen on his wife, and that his friend's wife was also very pretty, proposed (in the presence of both women, who had a say in this) that for a given portion of their journey they should swap wives. Every so often he remembers that he's supposed to be an iron merchant, and dutifully visits a foundry ("This part of the country is very rich in iron, but actually is so ugly that I had rather not talk about it").

In Tarascon his pocket is picked. In Bourges he gets lost at night in a labyrinth of twisting streets and, seeking directions to his hotel, the only man he finds to ask is "profoundly drunk". In Vannes he has to ask for directions again, a practice he hates: "Even if the man who answers me is only a little ridiculous or pompous, I think he is making fun of me." In Granville, a town characterised by "sombre gloom", he walks to a field surrounded by the sea on three sides and is told by a child who accompanies him: "You hear so often of the end of the world. Well, look. There it is."

In the provinces they don't even know how to die well: sobbing, wailing, the "terrible arrival" of the priest, the children marked for the rest of their lives by memories of horror and hysteria. In Paris, people just get it sensibly and quietly over with, no fuss. "Since the idea of *eternal* hell has left us, death has become a simple matter again, as it was before the reign of Constantine." As for an afterlife, he has "a young man from Grenoble" play with the idea of Paradise: first, health as good as he currently enjoys it; second, each year the wiping of Italy from his memory, so that each year for all eternity he can visit Milan, Florence, Rome, Naples as if for the first time. And third, the same, each month, for *Don Quixote* and *The Thousand and One Nights*.

Robert Adams, researching his book on Beyle in the 1950s, claims in his preface to that book that in an art gallery in Rome 'I ran into Beyle himself – bold, ironic, and broad-beamed, with receding hairline, wicked black sideburns, and his hands clasped behind his back; he was looking, appropriately, at a Coreggio.'

In August 2016 I saw Beyle in Notting Hill: unshaven, grey-green overcoat, sunglasses, boots, a floral-pattern shopping bag slung over his shoulder. He looked like a brigand. He crossed the road, I took a photograph, he vanished. The following month, I met a woman in Rome who told me that on a day in the 1990s she'd seen Roland Barthes on a train to Birmingham; he too was wearing an overcoat.°

On and off, I've been following Beyle for more than two decades. Beyle himself followed an actress to Marseilles with the approval of his father, who believed he was going to work for a grocer. His name, the one he's best known by and the one I'm not even sure I'm pronouncing right (Nabokov: 'One cannot hope to understand an author if one cannot even pronounce his name'), is an anagram of Shetland. The name of the young prostitute in London who promised

---

° The one, surely, he's wearing in the photograph of himself lighting a cigarette and captioned 'Left-handed' in *Roland Barthes par Roland Barthes*. Barthes was knocked down by a laundry van in a Paris street in February 1980 and died a month later from the injuries he sustained. On his desk at the time of his death he left the first pages of an essay he had just started, an essay on Beyle.

that if he'd take her with him to France she would cost him nothing, she would eat only apples, was Miss Appleby. He was short and overweight and after his hair fell out when he was young – a result of taking mercury as a treatment for syphilis – he wore a toupee. He was interested in the annual incomes of his friends and enemies and referred to money as it applied to himself as "fish". He saw the sea for the first time at the age of twenty-eight. He bungled things: while employed as a consul in Civitavecchia, he sent a letter in code to his employers in Paris and included the key to the code in the same envelope. He instructed that his autobiographical writing ("this excessive heap of Is and mes") should not be published until ten years after his death, and no one took any notice for several decades. In the unlikely event that he died rich, he wished to endow a literary prize for a work on "ambition, love, revenge, hatred, laughter, weeping, smiling, friendship, terror, hilarity" and "Which is the greatest comedian?" He kept a tally of his love affairs on his braces. He kept a plaster cast of Mathilde Dembowski's left hand on his writing desk. In the burnt-out ruins of Moscow in 1812 he met one of his early loves, now married to a general. He once went to Newcastle. He chased wild geese and red herrings. He barked up wrong trees. His handwriting was barely legible. He liked children (and wrote letters to a child who became Empress of the French and died in 1920 and is buried in Farnborough, Hampshire). He was so fond of using epigraphs from well-known authors that he habitually made them up. His funeral, according to Prosper Mérimée, was attended by three people. He wrote and rewrote his will (thirty-six versions in 1827 alone) without having anything of consequence to bequeath. A few books, a few clothes, an overcoat.

Another thing dying may be like (I keep a tally): leaving Rome by train. Here is how Elizabeth Bowen ends *A Time in Rome*: 'Such a day, when it does come, has nothing particular about it. Only from the train as it moved out did I look back at Rome. Backs of houses I had not ever seen before wavered into mists, stinging my eyes. My darling, my darling, my darling. Here we have no abiding city.'

In Rome, Beyle heard a scream in the street. Later that day, he noted – though death was hardly news, he'd served in the army, he'd ridden his horse over charred bodies – in the margin of his copy of *Promenades dans Rome*: "Sunday 6 April 34. A young girl murdered near me. I run up, she is in the middle of the street, at her head a little pool of blood, one foot in diameter." A little later, another marginal note: there was foam floating in the blood.

Carlo Emilio Gadda also noted that foam: 'the black foam of the blood almost clotted already; a mess! with some little bubbles still in the midst'. And adds, as writers do (the 'realist' ones: is there another kind?): 'like red-colored little maccheroni, or pink'.

In early 1840 Beyle fell into the fire by the chair where he was writing. He had his portrait painted in Rome and compiled a wish-list (a ring that when touched will cause a woman to fall in love with him, the ability to occupy two bodies at the same time, etc: see pages 91–2). By 1841, he is losing the faculty of speech: "A lapse lasts from six to eight minutes. The mind works satisfactorily, but without words." He has a stroke, a "grapple with the void", which he terms "disagreeable" (any fear or horror comes only "from all the silly nonsense that is put into our heads at the age of three"). In April, while lodging in Rome at number 48, Via Condotti, his boots are stolen by a servant but he refrains from accusing her because "I may be very sick in her house". He wants to be bled with leeches but the doctor refuses. "I consider that there is nothing ridiculous about dying in the street," he writes to a friend in Paris, "provided one does not do it on purpose."

Just a few hundred yards from the Via Condotti – up the Spanish Steps and turn right – Nikolai Gogol is writing *Dead Souls* ('O Russia, Russia!') and *The Overcoat* at number 125, Via Sistina.

In *Dead Souls*, Chichikov is conducting a financial scam, buying certificates of ownership of serfs who have recently died at knockdown prices from landowners who otherwise will be responsible for paying taxes on those serfs until the next census. As the owner of a significant number of serfs –

48 Via Condotti

dead or alive, no difference on paper – Chichikov will be able to get a government mortgage to buy property. In short, he calculates, for an investment of around 1,000 roubles he'll net around 200,000 roubles.

Gogol makes a point of not individuating Chichikov: 'He was neither too fat nor too thin, nor could he be described as either old or young.' He's the man on the Moscow suburban omnibus: 'I am sure the reader will be delighted to know that he unfailingly changed his underwear every other day and even every day during summer heatwaves, as the slightest unpleasantness offended him.' His one sartorial indulgence is a 'rainbow-colored scarf, a scarf of the sort that wives make with their own hands and give to their husbands with detailed instructions on how to wrap themselves up. As to bachelors, God only knows, I really cannot tell for sure who does it for them. I myself have never worn such a scarf.'

When they realise that he's up to something odd, the townsfolk can't get a fix on him: he's a con-man, or a spy, or a government agent, or a disgruntled veteran from the campaign of 1812, or even Napoleon in disguise, released from St Helena by the English – 'and therefore Chichikov wasn't really Chichikov at all'.

No rebel, Chichikov is as much a creature of the system as the other players he is pitching against; he is simply following the rules of the game through to their absurd conclusion. Or rather, inconclusion – because if in fact there is *no game being played*, and the rules are free-floating above a non-existent board, or if (same thing, in effect) the rules are so configured as to make the game unwinnable, there can be no ending.

Dead Souls – like Beyle's *Lucien Leuwen*, whose final part was planned to conclude with the reunion of estranged lovers in Rome – was never finished. In the decade following the publication of Part One, Gogol wrote and rewrote and rewrote Part Two, then burned the pages, took to his bed, refused all food, died.

The Overcoat tells of a meek copyist whose hard-won attainment of his dream, the purchase of a new overcoat, is met only with the usual indifference, corruption, violence. The birthday of Akaky Akakyevich is, Gogol decides – 'if my memory serves me right' – and it's a gratuitous detail, of no relevance to the plot – 23 March, which is the date on which Beyle will die.

On 22 March 1842, sometime after seven in the evening, Beyle collapses in the rue Neuve des Capucines in Paris.° He dies in the early hours of the following morning without regaining consciousness. A note in his pocket identifies him

---

° Also in 1842, Gogol's *Dead Souls* and *The Overcoat* are published. The latter ends with the ghost of the poor clerk seizing the overcoat of the boorish official who has refused to help him, and then vanishing, appeased ('evidently the Important Person's overcoat fitted him well'). And then – far too neat, stopping there – it ends again: there

as "Arrigo Beyle, Milanese"; three newspaper reports of his death spell his name wrong.

I think of Vallejo's poem – 'I will die in Paris, on a rainy day, on a day I can already remember . . .' – and of the sequence of photographs of a man dying in a Paris street taken by Brassaï from the window of an upper room overlooking the scene.

Daniil Kharms had a habit of lying down in the street and then, when a crowd had gathered to see what was wrong with him, getting up and walking away.

---

are reports from 'remote parts of the city' that the ghost is still active; a policeman claims to have seen it 'with his own eyes', though this one is different, 'much taller', and is clearly a different ghost. Possibly that of the original thief; not of Beyle, who was short. 'It was heading apparently towards Obukhov Bridge and presently disappeared completely in the darkness of the night.' Nabokov: 'Thus the story describes a full circle: a vicious circle as all circles are, despite their posing as apples, or planets, or human faces.'

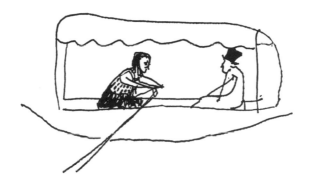

REFERENCES

Robert M. Adams, *Stendhal: Notes on a Novelist* (Merlin Press, 1959)

Robert Alter, *Stendhal* (Allen & Unwin, 1980)

Horst Bienek, *Bakunin: An Invention* (trans. Ralph R. Reid; Gollancz, 1977)

Roberto Bolaño, *Tres* (trans. Laura Healy; Picador, 2013)

Elizabeth Bowen, *A Time in Rome* (Vintage, 2003)

Andrew Brown, *Stendhal* (Hesperus, 2010)

Sophie Calle, *The Address Book* (trans. Pauline Baggio; Siglio, 2012)

— *Suite Vénitienne* (trans. Dany Barash and Danny Hatfield; Bay Press, 1988)

Emmanuel Carrère, *Limonov* (trans. John Lambert; Penguin, 2015)

Jean-Claude Carrière, *The Secret Language of Film* (trans. Jeremy Leggatt; Faber, 1995)

Machado de Assis, *A Chapter of Hats* (trans. John Gledson; Bloomsbury, 2008)

Marguerite Duras, *Roma*, in *Writing* (trans. Mark Polizzotti; University of Minnesota Press, 2011)

Ford Madox Ford, *The Bodley Head Ford Madox Ford*, vols. 1 and v (Bodley Head, 1962, 1971)

Carlo Emilio Gadda, *That Awful Mess on the Via Merulana* (trans. William Weaver; NYRB, 2007)

Nikolai Gogol, *Dead Souls* (trans. Andrew R. MacAndrew; New American Library, 1961)

— *The Overcoat* (trans. David Magarshack; W. W. Norton, 1965)

Alfred Hayes, *The Girl on the Via Flaminia* (Europa, 2007)

Giuseppe Tomasi di Lampedusa, 'Tutorials on Stendhal' (trans. David Gilmour), in *The Siren and Selected Writings* (Harvill Press, 1995)

Harry Mathews, *My Life in CIA* (Dalkey Archive, 2005)

— *Selected Declarations of Dependence* (Sun & Moon Press, 1996)

Vladimir Nabokov, *Nikolai Gogol* (New Directions, 1959)

Rainer Maria Rilke, *The Inner Sky* (trans. Damion Searls; David R. Godine, 2010)

— *Letters to a Young Poet* (trans. Charlie Louth; Penguin, 2011)

Viktor Shklovsky, *Zoo, or Letters Not about Love* (trans. Richard Sheldon; Dalkey Archive, 2001)

Jean Starobinski, 'Pseudonymous Stendhal', in *The Living Eye* (trans. Arthur Goldhammer; Harvard University Presss, 1989)

Stendhal, *The Abbess of Castro* (*L'Abbesse de Castro*; trans. C. K. Scott Moncrieff; Melville House, 2014)

— *Armance* (trans. C. K. Scott Moncrieff; Soho Book Company, 1986)

— *The Charterhouse of Parma* (*La Chartreuse de Parme*; trans. John Sturrock; Penguin, 2006)

— *Letters to Pauline* (trans. Andrew Brown; Hesperus, 2011)

— *The Life of Henry Brulard* (*La Vie de Henry Brulard*; trans. John Sturrock; Penguin, 1995)

— *Love* (*De l'Amour*; trans. Gilbert & Susanne Sale; Penguin, 1975)

— *Memoirs of an Egotist* (*Souvenirs d'Egotisme*; trans. David Ellis; Chatto & Windus, 1975)

— *Memoirs of a Tourist* (*Mémoires d'un Touriste*; trans. Allan Seager; Northwestern University Press, 1962)

— *The Red and the Black* (*Le Rouge et le Noir*; trans. Roger Gard; Penguin, 2002)

— *A Roman Journal* (*Promenades dans Rome*; trans. Haakon Chevalier; Orion Press, 1959)

— *Rome, Naples and Florence* (trans. Richard N. Coe; John Calder, 1959)

— *To the Happy Few: Selected Letters of Stendhal* (trans. Norman Cameron; John Lehmann, 1952)

— *Travels in the South of France* (*Voyage dans le midi de la France*; trans. Elisabeth Abbott; Calder and Boyars, 1971)

Michael Wood, *Stendhal* (Cornell University Press, 1971)

Ⓑeditions

Founded in 2007, CB editions publishes chiefly short
fiction (including work by Will Eaves, May-Lan Tan
and Diane Williams) and poetry (including Beverley
Bie Brahic, J. O. Morgan, D. Nurkse and Dan O'Brien).
Writers published in translation include Apollinaire,
Andrzej Bursa, Joaquín Giannuzzi, Gert Hofmann,
Agota Kristof and Francis Ponge.

Books can be ordered from www.cbeditions.com.